Peppermint Cocoa Crushes

CURL UP WITH ALL OF THE SWIRL NOVELS!

Pumpkin Spice Secrets by Hillary Homzie
Peppermint Cocoa Crushes by Laney Nielson
Cinnamon Bun Besties by Stacia Deutsch
Salted Caramel Dreams by Jackie Nastri Bardenwerper

PEPPERMINT COCOA CRUSHES

Laney Nielson

Sky Pony Press
New York

Sky Pony Press books may be purchased in bulk at special discounts for sales promotion, corporate gifts, fund-raising, or educational purposes. Special editions can also be created to specifications. For details, contact the Special Sales Department, Sky Pony Press, 307 West 36th Street, 11th Floor, New York, NY 10018 or info@skyhorsepublishing.com.

Sky Pony® is a registered trademark of Skyhorse Publishing, Inc.®, a Delaware corporation.

Visit our website at www.skyponypress.com.
Books, authors, and more at www.skyponypressblog.com
Visit the author's website at www.laneynielson.com.

10 9 8 7 6 5 4 3 2 1

Library of Congress Cataloging-in-Publication Data is available on file.

Cover design by Liz Casal
Cover photo credit: iStock

Paperback ISBN: 978-1-5107-3008-3
Ebook ISBN: 978-1-5107-3012-0

Printed in Canada

Chapter One
THE BEST NEWS

"Sasha!" Kevin and Karly sang as they leapt (literally) down the hall toward the cafeteria. "Sash-aaa!" Maybe it was a twin thing, maybe it was because they were my best friends, or maybe it was pure talent, but they had definitely perfected harmonizing my name. "Sash-aaa."

"Hey!" I called to them as I folded back the flaps of the box in front of me.

"Here." Mira handed me a can of tuna fish. Next to her, Anna inspected another one for dents. Other than us, the cafeteria was empty. Actually, the whole school was empty—dismissal had been about an hour ago, and things cleared out fast. Everyone was excited to start Thanksgiving vacation. Me? Not so much. I was glad we needed to stay late and wrap up the food drive.

Kevin cartwheeled toward the table, and Karly did a high kick. "We're here."

"I see that." I laughed as I loaded another can into the box. "Nice high kick, Karly."

"Thanks." She bowed. "I thought you'd appreciate it."

"You ready to work?" I glanced up at the clock. We had twenty minutes before the van from the food pantry would show up—twenty minutes to pack up two tables stacked high with cans and boxes.

"Yup, but first the good news," Kevin said. "Sash, you're going to love this. Ms. Kumar just told us."

Ms. Kumar was the faculty advisor for the Holidaze Spectacular—or, should I say, *The* Holidaze Spectacular. It's the middle school's annual talent show (and a big fund-raiser for a local cause). I'd been waiting to perform in it since forever. Well, since I was four years old. That was the first year Mom took me to the show, and when dancers appeared on stage, I stood up and began to twirl. Or so the story goes. That was the same year Dad gave me my first pair of ballet slippers. I was so excited, I wore them for an entire week, even in my sleep. That part I remember.

"Drumroll, please." With his hands, Kevin drummed the air.

"Just tell us already." Mira passed me another can.

"What is it?" Anna put her hands on her hips.

Karly stepped in front of her brother. "The director of the Summer Academy is going to judge the show this year."

"*The* Summer Academy?" I stopped working. "At the High School for Performing Arts in the city?"

"Yup." Kevin smiled.

The High School for Performing Arts had the best dance program in the state, probably in the country, and their Summer Academy for middle school students was super prestigious (as in, hard to get into). It was also super expensive (like, don't-even-think-about-it).

"Is there a prize?" Mira asked.

"That's the best part." Kevin smiled. "The first place winners get scholarships to the Summer Academy!"

"Wow." I tried to sound calm but inside, I was

jumping up and down. The chance to win a scholarship to the Summer Academy? That was the best news ever.

"That's some prize," Anna said, looking over at Kevin, Karly, and me. "You know, you guys are really good. You could win it."

"Uh, yeah." Kevin puffed up his chest. "Of course."

"You're so modest." Mira gave Kevin's arm a light punch.

"Hope the stage is big enough for your ego." Anna laughed.

"What can I say? I've got talent." Kevin dropped to the ground and did a fish flop. The four of us started to laugh.

Just then Ms. Medley, our principal, strode into the cafeteria. "How's it going?" She looked down at Kevin, who was flopping on the linoleum floor, and then back at us.

"Good." I glanced toward the loading dock beyond the cafeteria doors. I hoped the staff member from the food pantry didn't arrive early.

"Excellent!" Ms. Medley surveyed the boxes stacked by the door and then the cans on the table. "This is the most successful food drive we've ever had. Sasha, as the president this year, you've really put new life into the Community Service Club." She buttoned her coat and pulled her leather gloves from her pocket. "I'm impressed."

"Thanks," I said, smiling. I had worked hard on the food drive, and it was nice to be complimented on it.

Ms. Medley turned toward Karly. "And congratulations on Quiz Bowl. This is the first year we're sending a team to the televised tournament. I couldn't be prouder."

As Ms. Medley spoke, Karly's face dropped. Karly wasn't on the team that was going to the tournament. She was on the B team—or as she called it, the reject team.

"Actually, I'm not on the A team, so I won't be . . ." Karly's voice trailed off as Ms. Medley headed toward the exit; her heeled boots clacked across the linoleum floor. Then she stopped at the door and turned around.

"Sasha, tell Mr. Thomas when you're leaving," Ms. Medley said. Mr. Thomas was the assistant principal. "He's in the office. He's waiting for you to finish so he can lock up." Then she pushed open the door to the faculty parking lot. A blast of cold air hit me.

"You okay?" I said to Karly, stepping away from the table. She'd been really upset when she found out she wasn't going to the televised Quiz Bowl tournament.

"Yeah."

I put my arm around her. "I bet next year you're the captain of the A team."

"Thanks." She leaned her head on my shoulder. "That's what Ahmed said."

"See." I stepped back. "And Ahmed knows what he's talking about. He's super smart." Ahmed, an eighth grader, was the current captain of the Quiz Bowl A team.

"Super smart and super cute." Karly smiled.

"Wait . . . Ahmed? Super cute? What?"

"Shh." Karly pulled me away from the others. Then she leaned forward and whispered, "I have a crush on him."

"You have a crush on Ahmed?" I was surprised. Sure, we'd talked about liking boys before, but they were usually boys we didn't know, or didn't know well. There were boys at school (mostly eighth graders) we thought were cute. And Karly used to have a crush on her neighbor, but he was a high school junior, and I was pretty sure he didn't even know her name. Karly liking Ahmed was different. She was already friends with him.

"Shut up." Karly swatted my arm. "I don't want anyone else to know until I figure out if he likes me."

"O-kaaay." What if he liked her too? They could possibly *be* something, whatever that meant. I hadn't really thought about actually dating before.

"Who do *you* like?" Karly asked.

"Like? I don't like anyone."

Karly nudged my arm. "You sure about that?"

"I'm sure," I said, but I didn't feel so sure. From the way she was acting, it seemed like I was supposed to have a crush on someone too.

"Hey." Mira walked over to me. "Sash, I thought you said we didn't have a lot of time."

"We don't." I headed back to the table. "We need to get a move on it."

"How about some music?" Karly held up her phone and pressed the screen. Out came "The Dance of the Sugar Plum Fairy" from *The Nutcracker*.

"Seriously, Karly? You know I love Tchaikovsky, but we've got fifteen minutes to make this happen," Kevin said. He pushed back the sleeves of his sweatshirt and lifted an empty box onto the table. "We need some—"

"Fine." Karly pressed the screen of her phone and a pop song filled the air.

"Not my first choice, but I can work with it." Kevin dipped as he began loading boxes of pasta. I giggled, shimmying and bumping hips with Karly as Mira and Anna belted out the lyrics.

By the time the van from the food pantry pulled into the loading dock, all the boxes were packed.

"I've got to go," Mira said. "My cousins are coming."

"Me too." Anna looked down at her phone. "My dad wants me to clean my room before my grandmother arrives. Wish me luck. I haven't cleaned it since her last visit."

"Wasn't that, like, six months ago?" I asked.

Anna nodded. "It's not pretty. And I'm not proud of it."

"Good luck." I hugged Anna. "Thanks for helping, you guys."

"Anytime, Madame President," Mira said as we gave each other a side hug.

"Ha, ha." I handed Anna her mitten that had fallen

on the ground. "Don't forget we're doing the mitten and hat drive next month!"

"Got it." Mira wrapped her scarf around her neck.

Once the last box was loaded and the van pulled away, Kevin said, "You still want to do the Holidaze Spectacular routine together, right?"

"Yes," I said immediately. "Of course." Karly, Kevin, and I had made the decision months earlier. "Why?" I asked, suddenly uncertain. "Don't you?"

"I do!" He put up his hands as if I was accusing him of something. "It's just, now that the Summer Academy director will be the judge, the stakes are a lot higher . . . I wanted to make sure we're all in." He turned toward Karly. "You in?"

"Yup."

"Good," I said, tightening the elastic band around my ponytail. "Just think . . . if we win, all three of us get to go to the Summer Academy." Ever since Karly and Kevin and I started dancing at JayJay's Studio in third grade, we dreamed about dancing together at the Holidaze Spectacular and about going to the Summer Academy and then eventually all three of us going to the High School for Performing Arts. "We can do this."

"Definitely." Kevin looked down at his phone. "It's Mom," he said to Karly. "They're out front. The car's packed."

"Can I come?" I was joking. Sort of. But the truth was, hanging out with the Hall family at their grandparents' house sounded awesome, especially compared to the long, b-o-r-i-n-g weekend ahead of me. With my sister Claire in college in California, Thanksgiving was just going to be Mom and me. It wasn't that I didn't like doing stuff with Mom—I did. But she wasn't going to be doing anything other than her schoolwork. She'd already warned me about how much work she had. And the apartment still didn't really feel like home. And it was the first year I wasn't going to see Dad for Thanksgiving. And . . .

"It won't be so bad, Sash." Karly gave me a hug, a real one. "Just think—you can binge Netflix, no interruptions. And you can work on ideas for our routine. We're still good with our music choice, right?"

"Definitely," Kevin and I said at the exact same time.

"Listen to that: You're becoming one of us!" Karly said, and the three of us laughed.

"Happy Thanksgiving, Sash!" Kevin called as he headed toward the door.

Karly leaned toward me. "Text me."

"Of course."

"I'll be sure to give you updates on my crush." She waggled her eyebrows in a funny way. "And call when you want to talk about *your* crush! Okay?"

"Karly, I told you. I don't have a—"

"Come on, Sash. We're in seventh grade. You've got to like someone."

I do? I thought. But before I could say anything Karly sashayed out the door. "Love ya!" she called as the cold air hit me.

I headed down the hallway toward the main office to tell Mr. Thomas we were done. I thought about Karly liking Ahmed and how she thought I should have a crush too. It made sense, because Karly and I did everything together. We both got our ears pierced on her tenth birthday. We started on pointe on the same day. So if she liked a boy at school, then well, I probably should too.

When I passed the auditorium stage door, I stopped.

"Detour," I said aloud as I backed up.

There was no way I was passing up an empty stage.

The auditorium was dark and the air felt cold, as if the heat had been turned off hours earlier. I flipped on the lights. Ta-da! There it was, waiting for me.

I stood center stage, facing the rows of empty seats. I took off my coat, pulled out my phone and earbuds, and scrolled through my music until I found the song I wanted.

As the music flowed into my ears, I pliéed deeply. Keeping my shoulders back and my stomach tight, I turned . . . one, two, three pirouettes. I opened my arms and bent forward. Rising up, I turned my head stage right and then leapt across the stage.

I didn't think about what I was going to do next. I just danced. Free from worries and fears and what-ifs. Feeling the music, my body moved fast and slow, high and low through the space.

Then the song ended. I pulled out my earbuds and sat down on the stage, breathing deeply. *In thirty days, I will be here*, I thought. *Right here.* With Kevin and Karly and a packed audience. The lights will shine on us. The music will play. We will perform. And somewhere out there, the director of the Summer Academy will be deciding who will be given a scholarship.

When I stood up, I felt dizzy, like I'd done a turn without spotting. But I knew it wasn't from dancing. It was excitement. The Holidaze Spectacular would be the start of my dreams coming true.

But first I needed to survive Thanksgiving.

Chapter Two
NOT SO THANKFUL

"Mom, shouldn't we put the turkey in the oven or something?" It was eleven o'clock on Thursday morning and there wasn't a single Thanksgiving smell coming from the kitchen.

Mom sat at the dining room table, stacks of thick textbooks all around her. "About that . . ."

"About what? It's Thanksgiving. Please tell me we *are* going to have Thanksgiving dinner. Right?"

"Of course." She stood up and walked to the kitchen.

I followed her. The only thing on the stove was the kettle, still steaming from the cup of tea she'd recently made. I opened the oven door—nothing inside. "Mom, where's all the food? We need to start the turkey."

"I thought this year we could simplify things." Mom opened the fridge.

Simplify things? I peered over her shoulder. All I saw were a bunch of pint-sized plastic containers. My heart sank.

"Market Stop had a great deal on Thanksgiving dinners."

"Mom." I was pretty close to tears. "But what about our special stuffing?"

She pointed to a plastic container on the top shelf. It was labeled: IN-HOUSE STUFFING. Whose house? *Not ours*, I wanted to say, but instead I asked, "And our pecan pie?"

"Well, that, of course, we're going to make. From scratch. Right now." Mom pulled out the butter. "You get the flour."

I opened up the cabinet and grabbed the ingredients. I was still mad about Thanksgiving being such a fail, but standing next to Mom in the kitchen, working the chunks of butter into the flour, I started to feel a little better.

"Sash, it's not always going to be like this."

"I know," I said, but I wasn't so sure. Ever since the divorce, Mom kept saying that, but between Mom going back to school and Claire and Dad moving to California, the "this" just kept changing.

"In June, I'll graduate. Then I'll get a good job. We'll go on vacation." Mom flicked flour at me.

I ducked, the flour dusting the top of my hair.

"A vacation," she repeated. "Doesn't that sound good?"

Talking about going on vacation was pretty much Mom's favorite subject. "Yeah." I flicked flour at her.

"Where should we go?" She wiped the flour off her nose. "Somewhere warm?"

"Disney World. Definitely."

"You got it."

Later in the afternoon when the pie was cooling, Mom pulled the plastic containers from the fridge. I held the plates as she scooped the grocery store-made mashed potatoes and wiggled the green beans onto our plates. I poured some gravy on the already-cooked slices of turkey, and we took turns microwaving.

"Okay . . . so it's not exactly Pinterest-worthy." Mom lifted a fork to her mouth. "But the cranberry sauce is pretty good!"

"But it's not great." I put my fork down. "Mom, no matter what, we're cooking next year, okay?"

"Deal," Mom said.

Of course, the best part of Thanksgiving was the pecan pie. Mom bought vanilla ice cream and whipped cream and we piled both on our plates of pie. I bit into the gooey sweet pecans and immediately felt happy. If Thanksgiving had a taste, it was our pecan pie.

After that, we called Claire. My sister was in her first semester of college, and Mom and I both missed her. A lot. It was her first Thanksgiving away. She'd been gone since the end of August, and she wasn't coming home until the third week in December. Right in time to see me perform in the Holidaze Spectacular.

Mom and I took turns talking, and then we put her on speakerphone so she could tell us about her bus ride to Dad's. She'd sat next to a Harry Styles impersonator who insisted on singing the entire five hours and giving everyone his fake autograph. By the time Claire handed the phone to Dad, Mom and I were laughing hard.

"Hey, Dad." I took him off speakerphone. It wasn't like my parents couldn't talk. They were divorced, not dead to each other, but in my mind, I kept them in separate places. It was like how I loved mashed potatoes and I loved cranberry sauce (well, not from Market Stop, but normally)—I loved them equally but I didn't want them touching on my plate. Okay, bad analogy. Point is, Mom and Dad didn't go together anymore, and it made me feel less sad when I could compartmentalize them.

Mom started on the dishes. With the phone to my ear, I walked to my room and closed the door. "Dad, I miss you."

"And I miss you. Claire told me you're doing the show. I'm so proud of you, Sash. We need to get someone to take a video of it."

"I'm sure Mrs. Hall will."

"You're right. She'll probably upload it to YouTube. And then you'll go viral." Dad paused. "I can't wait for you to visit. Claire says you're going to want to turn my studio into a dance studio."

"Probably. It's pretty hard practicing in the apartment. Our downstairs neighbor doesn't seem to appreciate my jumps."

Dad laughed. "I guess you'll need to head to JayJay's to practice the power moves."

"Hey, Dad. I wanted to ask you about that. Mom said she wasn't sure if we had the money to cover next semester's dance classes. I was wondering if maybe I could have them as my Christmas gift." I felt bad that the classes were expensive. With the divorce, and with both Mom and Claire in school, money was tight.

"That sounds like a good idea. Let me talk to the North Pole—" He coughed. "I mean, Ms. Claus, and see what we can come up with."

After I hung up with Dad, I felt sad. California was far away. Like 2,703 miles away. And sometimes after talking to Claire or Dad it felt even farther.

I crashed on my beanbag chair and looked up at my poster of the Alvin Ailey Dance Company. I'd picked it out when Dad took me to see a performance for my birthday last year. That was before he moved to California. We'd spent the whole day in the city. Dad had even taken a picture of me on the steps of the High School for Performing Arts. Shoot! I'd forgotten to tell Dad that the winners of the Holidaze Spectacular win scholarships to the Summer Academy. He would think that was cool.

I picked up my phone, ready to call him back,

but an incoming text from Karly distracted me. She wanted my advice about whether she should text Ahmed and wish him a happy Thanksgiving. What was happening to Karly? That was the third Ahmed-related text she'd sent me in the last three hours.

I texted back: *I guess.* Then she was gone, and I was left thinking about what she'd said the day before: "You've got to like *some*one."

Okay, maybe. But who?

I looked down at my phone—a snap from Kevin (we were on a streak). There he was: eating pecan pie, whipped cream on his nose. It was so Kevin. I went into the kitchen and took a picture of our half-eaten pie and sent it to him.

On Saturday, Mom and I headed to the Senior Center. That's where Karly and I usually volunteered with the lunch program, but with Karly out of town, Mom said she would come. Actually, Mom was the reason Karly and I started volunteering there. Before Mom went back to school, she was, like, Volunteer of the Year.

Both Miss Melinda and Big T, who were regulars

at the Saturday lunch program, gave me a hug. Big T hadn't met Mom before because he started coming to the Senior Center after she stopped volunteering. He made a big deal about meeting her.

"You've got a special daughter," Big T said. "She always brings me extra butter for my rolls. And the biggest slice of cake." Big T winked at me.

"That's nice," Mom said, smiling and sitting down next to Miss Melinda. "Can I help you with that?" She pointed to a piece of chicken on Miss Melinda's plate.

"I've got it." Miss Melinda picked up her fork and knife. "But Missy over at Table Ten could probably use your help."

When Mom stood up, I sat down.

"Good." Miss Melinda glanced behind her. "She's gone. You know, I prefer young people."

I laughed.

"How are *you*?" She put down her utensils and leaned toward me. "Any new boyfriends?"

"No." Every week, Miss Melinda asked about boyfriends and every week I laughed and told her I didn't have any. But that day I didn't laugh. Why was everyone so boy-crazy?

"Are you sure?" Miss Melinda said. "When I was your age, I had so many crushes."

"Would you like some more green beans?" I asked, wanting to change the subject.

Before we left, Mom and I stopped by the director's office. Mom wanted to say hello and I wanted to tell her the date had been set for the Holidaze Spectacular. The Senior Center usually provided transportation for anyone who wanted to attend.

"That's great, Sasha. We could use something to look forward to around here."

"Is everything okay?" Mom asked.

"Budget cuts." The director picked up the calculator on her desk. "It looks like we won't have enough money to continue our meals program." The center served free and reduced rate lunches daily, plus they delivered meals to housebound seniors.

"That's terrible," I said, thinking about Miss Melinda and Big T. I knew they not only looked forward to the meals, they counted on them. "What can we do?"

"I don't know," she said, sounding like she'd already given up.

I don't know? What kind of answer was that?

Chapter Three

WINTER DREAMS

By Sunday, I was bored. Beyond bored. I'd binge-watched anything worth bingeing. I'd scrolled through Instagram trying to find a boy, maybe a friend of a friend, worth crushing on, but I gave up after I'd seen the same turkey meme five times. I'd also stalked the High School for Performing Arts website, watching the Summer Academy promo video until I knew every word. And I'd written a detailed rehearsal schedule for Kevin, Karly, and me.

So by midmorning Sunday, I was sitting at the dining room table sketching costume ideas for our Holidaze Spectacular act, waiting for Kevin and Karly to come home. Our dining room table still looked awkward in the apartment. In our old house it had had its own room, but in the apartment it took up half the living space and had turned into the every-thing-table. It was where Mom studied, where we folded laundry, where I did my homework.

"Did you sign up for the coding workshop I told you about?" Mom looked up from her laptop. "It's at the library, Saturday afternoons, starting in January."

"No." Under the table, I flexed my left foot and then my right.

"Why not?"

I picked up a red pencil. "I don't think I can fit it in, not with my dance schedule."

"But Sasha. If you want to apply to Tech Magnet for high school, you need to start filling your resume with STEM-related activities."

I don't want to go to Tech Magnet, I wanted to say, but instead I folded in my lips and colored the tutu I'd sketched in my pad.

"Have you looked into the robotics club at school yet?"

"No." I held up the pad, blocking my view of Mom. I'd drawn a candy cane—striped tutu—very festive.

Karly would love it! Now I needed to think about Kevin's costume.

"You know, Claire did the robotics club in middle school." Mom pushed her screen down and looked over at me.

"Mom, I know." Claire did a lot of things I didn't do. I dropped my sketchpad on the table.

"Sash, I know it seems like a long time away, but before you know it you'll be applying to college and—"

"Mom, I'm in seventh grade." I didn't want to go to Tech Magnet. They didn't even have a dance program.

But Mom had the whole thing mapped out, and she was definitely using Claire's map—the one where Claire went to Tech Magnet and ended up with a scholarship to college.

Zzz. Zzz. My phone vibrated.

"Is it Claire?" Mom asked.

I looked down at the screen. "No. It's Karly." It was the text I'd been hoping for since I woke up. Karly and Kevin were home from their grandparents'. Finally!

"Go," Mom said before I even asked. She knew I'd been waiting all weekend to rehearse with them. We now had only twenty-four days to get ready for the Holidaze Spectacular. Not that I was counting or anything.

"Thanks." I stuffed my sketchpad into my dance bag and headed over to the closet.

"You need a hat," Mom said as I zipped up my coat. "And mittens."

I grabbed the mittens but I couldn't find a hat. "I'll be fine," I said.

"Call me if you need a ride." Mom's eyes were back on the screen, her fingers flying across the keyboard.

"Okay." I took my phone and pressed my earbuds into place.

"Be careful," Mom said without looking up at me. "Watch out for cars," she called as I opened the door.

I ran down the flight of stairs, the music thudding in my ears. When I pushed open the front door of our building, the cold hit me. Mom was right—I needed a hat.

I headed down the street, my head bopping to the music. On the corner of Main and Walnut, outside Sugarman's Market, I did a fouetté. Then, watching my reflection in the store's window, I did a hitch kick. Not bad. At the crosswalk, I looked both ways and then leapt. Two stag leaps and I was on the other side of the street. That was one good thing about moving into the apartment. We were closer to the center of town, so I could walk (or dance) almost everywhere—the studio, school, Karly and Kevin's.

"Sasha!" Mrs. Hall hugged me as I stepped inside their warm house.

"Did you have a good turkey day?" Mr. Hall called from the living room where he was putting a log on the fire.

"Pretty good, thanks." I pulled off my sneakers and lined them up next to the collection of shoes by the door. "How was your trip?"

"Well," Mrs. Hall said. "Let's just say I can sing 'Snow, Snow, Baby!' in my sleep." Smiling, I stuffed my mittens into my coat. "Snow, Snow, Baby!" was the song Karly, Kevin, and I had chosen for our routine.

"Snow, snow, baby!" Mr. Hall sang, swinging his hips wildly, flapping his arms, and waving his hands.

I laughed. "I guess it was a long car ride."

"Very," Mrs. Hall said as I headed down the front hall to hang up my coat. "You know where they are."

"Thanks." I opened the door to the basement.

"Sasha!" Karly called from below.

On the fifth step from the bottom, I jumped.

"Sa-sha. Sa-sha," Kevin chanted as if I was a quarterback after a winning play. Enthusiasm was one of the things I loved about the Hall family. It must've been in their DNA.

Another thing I loved about the Hall family was their basement.

It was a dance studio.

"Hey guys." I sashayed across the top-of-the line hardwood sprung flooring Mr. Hall had installed himself. Pulling on the barre above them, Kevin and Karly stood.

"What's up?" I could see my reflection in the mirror behind them. And my hair was a mess. I took the elastic band off my wrist and pulled my hair into a high ponytail.

"Bad news," Karly said.

"Oh no." My mind raced with what it could be—the Holidaze Spectacular was cancelled . . . our performance was cut . . . the director of the Summer Academy pulled out . . .

"We need a new song," Kevin said.

"What? Why?"

"Have you heard my dad sing it?" Karly shuddered. "He kind of ruined it for me."

"Yup." Kevin swayed and waved his hands, imitating what I had seen Mr. Hall do upstairs. No, actually, Kevin's version was mild compared to Mr. Hall's. "Once we heard him sing it, we realized it was kind of a corny song."

"Okay, okay." I laughed as Kevin belted out the chorus. "Maybe that song wasn't the best choice. What're you thinking?"

"I like 'Snow and Ice.'" Kevin started tutting—raising his arms up, bending in his wrists, forming right angles.

Karly groaned. "I don't want to do all hip-hop." She lifted her leg onto the barre. "I think we should do 'Snowland.'" She brought her arms up over her head and reached toward the mirror.

"No way," Kevin said. "I want to show off some of my new acro moves, and 'Snowland' would be all ballet. Bor-ing."

"How about 'Winter Dreams'?" I turned toward Kevin. "We could incorporate some of your new stunts, maybe your one-handed front walkover."

He smiled. "I'm getting pretty good at it, aren't I?" He poked me in the stomach.

"Definitely." I reached for the barre.

"Don't feed his ego." Karly dropped her leg onto the ground. "Hmm . . . 'Winter Dreams' . . . I can work with that." She plugged her phone into the speaker on the floor. "Let's free dance and see what we come up with."

"Sounds good." As the song filled the basement, I spread open my arms and tilted my head back.

Karly put the song on repeat, and we danced to it over and over. I lost myself in the music, and then Karly and I danced side by side, mirroring our moves and building off each other's ideas. We belted out the refrain. Kevin started singing too.

"What do we think?" Karly stopped the music.

"It's perfect." Kevin winked at me. "Summer Academy, here we come."

"Not quite," I said. "First we need to choreograph it."

We spent the next hour sharing ideas and demonstrating to each other what we were thinking. It was slow work, but we were getting there, and by the time my phone rang, we'd nailed down the opening section.

It was Mom calling and asking me to pick up milk on the way home.

"I should go," I said to Karly and Kevin. "But I'll work on it some more."

"Me too," Karly said.

"I almost forgot." I dug through my dance bag for the rehearsal schedule I'd come up with. "Here." I handed Kevin and Karly a printout of the month of December with our practice times on it. "Take a look. But I think it should work."

"Thanks." Karly waved the paper in the air. "And I like the costume ideas you texted me. We'll need to buy the materials soon."

"This weekend."

Kevin wrinkled up his nose. "No tutus for me, okay?" His eyes sparkled.

Outside, the temperature had dropped. The wind stung my face. I covered my ears with my mittened hands. But I didn't care how cold it was. I was thinking about Kevin.

Kevin!

Why hadn't I thought of it before? He was the perfect person for me to have a crush on. We liked all the same stuff, plus we were already friends. Best friends. I'd never really thought about it before, but

Kevin was cute. Wasn't he? In a goofy, hair flopping, sometimes-smelly-feet kind of way.

Yeah, Kevin was the obvious answer.

By the time I reached Sugarman's Market, my toes were freezing, my ears were numb, and my head was filled with reasons why Kevin was a good choice for my crush. When I opened the door, the bells hanging from the wooden doorknob jangled merrily. Even in the summer, the sound of them made me think of sleigh bells.

"Hello, Sasha," Mr. Sugarman called from behind the antique cash register with its mechanical keys and brass money drawer.

"Hi, Mr. Sugarman!" I smiled, relaxing into the warmth of the store. It was one of the few places in town that never changed. Other stores might go out of business or expand, but not the market. Mr. Sugarman was definitely an "If it ain't broke don't fix it" kind of person. I liked that about him. And I liked everything about the store, especially the smell: fresh-baked chocolate chip cookies. Mr. Sugarman made them every afternoon, just in time for the after-school crowd.

I was headed toward the refrigerated case when I

heard Mira's laugh coming from the back of the store. I did a pivot turn and hurried down the aisle lined with jars of peanut butter and dusty soup cans to the café area. Maybe café was too fancy a word for the three tables with mismatched chairs set up in the back, but it was cozy, and one of our favorite places to hang.

"Hi," I said as Mira and Anna came into view.

"Hey, Sash." Mira waved to me from the center table.

"Look at your nose," Anna said. "It's bright red."

I touched the cold tip.

"You're freezing," Mira said. "Sit down." She pushed her mug toward the empty chair. "Have a sip."

Smelling the sweet cocoa, I plopped down in the seat and pulled off my mittens, placing them on the table. I warmed my hands on Mira's mug. Then I took a sip.

Delicious.

I slid the mug back toward her. "Thanks," I said, unzipping my coat.

"Sasha, you want something?" Mr. Sugarman called from behind the counter.

"Yes, please." I pulled out my wallet and walked over.

"Hey," I said as I passed Pete, who was pouring sugar into a dispenser. Pete was in my math class. He'd moved to town to live with his grandparents (Mr. and Mrs. Sugarman) a couple of months ago. I knew he was on the boys' basketball team at school. But I didn't know him. Not really.

"Sasha." He wiped his hands on the white half-apron tied around his waist. "Hi."

"Do you want to try the flavor of the day?" Mr. Sugarman asked when I reached the counter. "Candy Cane Cocoa." He nodded toward his grandson. "Pete came up with it."

"That sounds good."

I watched as Mr. Sugarman poured the hot chocolate, flicked in a dash of peppermint, swirled whipped cream on it, and then sprinkled crushed candy canes on top.

"Wow. Thanks."

After I paid, I sat back down with Mira and Anna.

"Fancy." Mira dipped her finger into the whipped cream rising up from my mug. "Crushed candy canes. Nice touch." She licked her finger. "I told you we should've ordered it," she said to Anna. "But nooo, you didn't want to try something new. Only basic hot chocolate for you."

I laughed. Sometimes the two of them reminded me more of squabbling siblings than the best friends they were. Then I took a sip.

Yum.

The peppermint and the chocolate were perfect together.

"Sash, you need to help me decide what to do for the Holidaze Spectacular. Because she's been zero help." Anna pointed at Mira and stuck out her tongue.

"What?" I asked. "I thought you were going to dance."

"I don't know. I was thinking . . . with you, Kevin, and Karly dancing, I might stand out more if I did something else."

"You should play the piano," I said. Truth was, Anna was a great dancer, but she was an even better pianist.

"That's what I said." Mira leaned back in her chair.

"Yeah." Anna turned toward Mira. "That's what you said *after* you told me to juggle, do stand-up comedy, and perform a cheer routine."

"No cheer routine." I shook my head, my ponytail swinging behind me. "Play the piano. You'll be awesome. But not too awesome, I hope," I said, smiling, and then drinking more of the sweet cocoa. My toes started to warm up.

"Mira's doing a new spoken word poem."

"That's great." I turned toward Mira, who gave me an exaggerated thumbs-up.

"We're not expecting to win," Anna said. "We just want to have fun."

"Speak for yourself." Mira swatted Anna's hand. "How's your routine coming, Sasha?"

"Pretty good. We just started working on it."

"Hey." Mira leaned forward. "What do you think about Karly's crush?"

"She told you?" What happened to Karly being all secretive about it?

"Yeah, she called me. She wanted to know if she should text him 'Happy Thanksgiving.'"

"She called you?" She'd only texted me.

"Yeah, I guess she wanted to talk to someone with experience."

"Seriously?" Anna rolled her eyes. "Going out with

Ben for two days in sixth grade doesn't exactly qual-
ify you as a relationship expert."

"Whatever." Mira turned toward me. "They'd
make a cute couple, don't you think?"

"I guess." I took another sip.

"Anywho." Anna smiled at me. "Who do you like?"

"Uh." I put the mug down and shook my head.

"You're keeping it secret, aren't you?" She smiled.
"Good idea."

"What are you talking about?" Mira said. "Sasha
doesn't have time for boys."

"Mmm-hmm." I crunched on a piece of candy
cane. I was *not* going to share my thoughts about
Kevin. Not yet.

Just then Mira's cell phone rang, playing "Jingle
Bells." Anna grabbed hers too—they were always
changing their ringtones to be the same tune.

With a spoon, I swiped the whipped cream off
the top of my cocoa. Mira talked to her mom on the
phone, and Anna checked her texts.

"Gotta go." Mira stood up. "My cousins don't leave
until tomorrow. And Mom says they're climbing the
walls without me to play with. I can't believe I used to

beg my parents to have another kid." She zipped up her coat. "It's only been four days, and I'm so over it."

"I've got to go, too." Anna slipped her phone into her coat pocket. "Last family dinner before my grandmother leaves."

The bells on the door jangled as Mira and Anna left the store. I took another sip and then picked up my phone. There was a snap from Kevin—a photo of his half-eaten dinner. I took a photo of the inside of my mug—an inch of cocoa left with a few specks of crushed candy canes. If the Halls were already eating dinner, it meant I should get going.

After I grabbed a quart of milk from the case, I headed over to Mr. Sugarman, who stood behind his old-fashioned cash register. "How's life treating you, Sasha?" He punched a few of the rounded keys.

"Pretty good." I zipped up my coat.

Mr. Sugarman handed me the bagged milk. "Stay warm out there."

"Thanks!" I headed toward the door.

"Wait up!" Pete called.

When I turned around, he was walking over to me, holding my mittens.

"Here you go." He handed them to me. "They were on the table."

"Thanks," I said, putting them on. "It's cold out there."

"Yeah. They're predicting a really cold December." Pete started to turn away from me.

"Hey, the Community Service Club is organizing a hat and mitten drive for the holidays. You could help. I mean, uh, if you want to. We could use help," I said, suddenly feeling very warm.

He wiped his hands on his apron. "Sure."

"Great!" I said, then started babbling. "Of course, I'm even more excited for the Holidaze Spectacular, which is going to be awesome. The first meeting for that is tomorrow." I pulled at the collar of my coat. "You should come, if you're interested."

"Performing's not really my thing." He shuffled his feet. A dusting of flour, or maybe it was powdered sugar, coated his sneakers.

"There's other stuff involved besides just performing." I unzipped my coat. "Tech. Backstage help . . ."

"Okay, maybe. I need to check my game schedule." He looked down, then up at me. "Have you studied for the math quiz?"

"Is that tomorrow?" I was surprised. I never forgot tests or assignments. My color-coded weekly planner pretty much guaranteed I stayed on top of everything.

"Mrs. Giberga postponed it a few times, but yeah, I'm pretty sure it's tomorrow."

"It's all the geometry terms from chapter ten, right?"

"Yup." He looked down at his apron again. "I made some flashcards on QuizTime. If you want, you could use them to study."

"That would be great, actually. Thanks!" I turned toward the door. "Tests the first day back after vacation should be against the law or something. Don't you think?"

Pete laughed. I opened the door, making the bells jangle. I smiled.

Chapter Four
THE CLUES

"Thanks for picking up the milk," Mom said as I hung up my coat. She sat at the dining room table, the same place she'd been when I left. Only one thing had changed: Her stacks of books and papers had multiplied. "Did you have fun?"

"It was good. We worked on our routine." I put the milk in the fridge and opened the freezer. "What's for dinner?" I asked, checking out our selection of frozen entrees: veggie pizza, mac and cheese, and corn dogs. Hmm . . .

"How about French toast?" Mom stood up, stretching her arms over her head and clasping her hands.

"I think there's some bacon in the fridge, too." She leaned to one side and then the other.

I shut the freezer. "Breakfast for dinner. My fav!" I was glad we were taking a break from frozen food. The corn dogs looked like they had freezer burn anyway.

After we ate, I headed to my room to study for the math quiz (thank you, Pete Sugarman). Usually I studied at the dining room table, but I didn't want Mom to launch into a lecture about how important it was for me to keep my math grade up. I knew she was worried my ninety-four would slip and that would lower my chance of getting into Tech Magnet.

I did a couple of rounds of the QuizTime flash cards. Then I took the practice quiz. I scored a one hundred. *Bam.* Perfect.

So when Kevin texted me, I stopped studying. He sent me a photo of Karly reading, and we texted back and forth about costume ideas. I was getting into the idea of *like* liking him. But how could I figure out if he *like* liked me? That was the next step, right?

I needed advice. But I couldn't exactly call my BFFs. Kevin was out for obvious reasons. As for Karly, I knew that she was currently trying to do the same thing— figure out if Ahmed liked her—but if I asked her, it would just turn into her wanting to know who I liked, and me liking her brother might seem too weird. I didn't want to go there until I knew he liked me too.

Plus, I could use someone with experience—more experience than Mira and her sixth-grade, forty-eight-hour "boyfriend."

I needed Claire.

"What's up, Sash?" Claire said on the other end of the phone. She was back in her dorm room in California, having survived the bus ride from Dad's— no impersonators on the return trip.

"I think I . . . I like Kevin." It was the first time I'd said the words out loud. And to be honest, they sounded more than a little weird.

"Of course you like Kevin. He's your best friend."

"No. I *like* like him."

"Oh," Claire said.

"What does that mean?"

"I just never imagined you and Kevin as anything more than friends."

"Whatever." Her comment annoyed me. I'd forgotten the downside of having an older sister—her know-it-all, slightly superior attitude. But I ignored it. I needed her help.

"How will I know if he *like* likes me back?"

"You'll know."

Sometimes Claire could be so unhelpful. "But *how*?"

"There'll be clues."

Clues? What was Claire talking about? What was this—the Nancy Drew guide to crushes?

"Like what? What kind of clues?"

I heard another voice in the background on Claire's end of the phone. Then Claire said, "Sorry, Sash. I've got to go. Elena's home." Elena was her roommate.

Hearing my sister call her dorm room "home" made me feel sort of sad. Claire had already found a new place where she belonged, while I still didn't feel like the apartment was home.

"Bye," I said, but she was already gone.

Claire had been less helpful than I'd hoped. So I Googled: "How do you know if a boy likes you?"

I was relieved when tons of quizzes and articles popped up. It always made me feel more normal when the thing I was searching was something other people also wanted to know.

I grabbed a pad and pen and jotted down notes as I read through a few sites. If it had misspellings or typos, I went to the next site. I needed credible sources. Or at least, people who could spell. (Our school librarian had done a lesson on fake news. Spelling errors were definitely a red flag.) I found a quiz called "Are You a Perfect Match?" But I gave up after the third question: Do your knees wobble when he stands near you?

Uh, no.

This was Kevin we were talking about, not some movie star. Plus, I was pretty sure people's knees didn't wobble, not in real life.

The best article I found was on a teen fashion magazine site:

How Do You Know If He/She Likes You?

I wrote down a bunch of points. Then I closed all the tabs and looked over my notes. Within five minutes, I created a Google doc:

The Clues
He calls or texts you.
He tries to make you laugh.
He stares at you.
He teases you.
He compliments you.
He tries to impress you.

As I typed the last clue, my phone rang.

It was Kevin. I glanced up at my list—the first clue: *He calls or texts you.* Uh, check.

"Hi," I said, suddenly feeling self-conscious.

"Hey," he said. "You know we have a math quiz tomorrow?"

"Yeah." I felt bad that I hadn't reminded *him* when Pete first reminded me. Kevin bombed the last quiz, and I knew he wanted to get his math grade back up. "Pete Sugarman made some flash cards on QuizTime. You could use them to study."

"I would, but Karly is forcing me to make flash cards. You know, the paper kind. She says the only way to get the terms in my brain is to draw them."

I laughed.

He cleared his throat, then said, "Umm, when did you see Pete?"

Why was Kevin asking? Could he be jealous? One of the websites had mentioned jealousy could be a sign of interest. "At Sugarman's. I ran into Mira and Anna there, too."

"Did Anna tell you she's going to play piano at the Holidaze Spectacular?"

"Yeah," I said. "She'll be great."

"Yup, but not as great as us. Right?"

"Right."

"Okay, Sash. I should go. I need to find some index cards. How many terms are there anyway?"

"Like twenty-five."

"Seriously? Ouch. If I end up hospitalized with a hand-cramp, please tell me you'll come visit."

"Of course I will," I said, and then laughed.

After the call ended, I opened my Google doc and looked over my list of clues.

He calls you. Check.

He tries to make you laugh. Definitely. Check.

So far, not bad. I'd been tracking clues for less than five minutes and I'd already checked off two out of the six, but I needed six out of six. I wouldn't take the next step (whatever that was) until I was one hundred percent sure.

Brushing my teeth, I thought about school the next day. It might've been a slow Thanksgiving break, but I knew everything was about to speed up, and I was glad. I'd much rather be busy than bored.

There was the math quiz first period, then the organizational meeting for the Holidaze Spectacular at lunch. After school, I had ballet at JayJay's (my

dance bag was already packed) but before I left
school, I needed to check in with Mr. Thomas about
where the Community Service Club could set up for
the mitten and hat drive. I'd found a neon pink tree
in the theater room that I wanted to use to hang the
donations. It would definitely get people's attention!

Then later, Karly, Kevin, and I were going to choreograph our routine. If we had a shot at winning the
Summer Academy scholarships, we needed to stick
to my rehearsal schedule: three hours a day, five days
a week. Plus, I had homework and end of the semester
tests. Like always, I was shooting for straight A's. And
then there was the Kevin project—I wanted to ace that
too!

Chapter Five
FIFTY-FIFTY

"Isn't that awesome about Karly?" Anna asked.

"What?" I sat down in my usual seat next to Anna in math class. It was first period and my toes were still cold from walking to school. "What's going on?"

"Awkward." Anna paused. "I thought she would've told you first."

"Tell me what?"

"It's her news. She should tell you."

Annoyed, I turned to face Kevin who was sitting on my other side. "What's up with Karly?"

"I'll tell you later." Kevin didn't look up at me. He was flipping through his flash cards.

"Come on." I tapped the side of his desk. "What is it?"

Then Mrs. Giberga cleared her throat. "Good morning, class."

"Later," Kevin whispered as he wrapped the index cards with a rubber band and dropped them into his backpack.

Right then I wasn't thinking about Kevin and my checklist of whether he liked me or not. I was thinking about what Karly's good news could be and why she hadn't told me first. Besides Kevin, *I* was the person she told stuff to. Not Anna. Not Mira. Me. When she didn't make the Quiz Bowl A team back in September, she'd told me right away, and I was pretty sure I was the first to know about her crush on Ahmed. Maybe that was it? Maybe Ahmed had asked her out? But there was no way Karly would tell Anna before she told me. Then I remembered Karly called Mira over Thanksgiving break for advice. My stomach dropped. Maybe I was wrong.

"Nothing says 'Vacation's over' like a test." Mrs. Giberga stood at the top of my row and handed Pete, who sat in the front, a stack of tests. A couple of kids groaned. When Pete turned around to hand the tests to the kid sitting behind him, he glanced back at me. I mouthed *"Thank you."*

After class, Kevin and I walked down the hall together like we always did. He had social studies next and I had science, but we were headed in the same direction.

"So what's the big news?" I asked.

"Karly got on the A team."

"For Quiz Bowl?"

"Yup. She's going to the televised tournament."

"That's awesome. But I thought—"

"Sara Burke, you know . . . the cocaptain? She couldn't go. Her grandparents are having a big fiftieth anniversary party out of state somewhere on the same day. So the team voted on who to take from the B team, and Karly was chosen."

"That's great. She must be so psyched!" I paused outside the door to Kevin's social studies classroom. "But why didn't she tell me?"

"Well." He hesitated. "It's just . . ."

"It's just what?"

"Gotta go." He stepped into the classroom.

There was definitely something Kevin didn't want

to tell me. "Don't forget the meeting in Ms. Kumar's room," I called after him. "At lunch."

"Got it." He waved.

I ran-walked the rest of the way to science, thinking about Karly. I was happy for her, but I was hurt she hadn't texted or called to tell me. Entering the science lab, I slowed down as I headed over to Mira and Karly, who were setting out the materials we needed for the lab.

"Hey." I put my binder down on the table.

"Hey Sasha," Mira said. "Did you hear Karly's going to be a TV star?"

I turned toward Karly. She was looking down at the beaker in her hand. Her face reddened.

"Yeah." I wanted to sound normal, but I sounded angry. "Why didn't you tell me?"

"I didn't want you freaking out." She put the beaker down and looked up at me.

"Why would I freak out?"

"Because it's in two weeks, five days before the Holidaze Spectacular."

"Oh." Karly was right—inside, I started freaking out.

"The next couple of weeks are going to be really intense. I have to practice every day with the team and study a lot." She glanced up at Ms. Stone, who was making her way toward us. "The tournament is going to be live streamed and on the local station."

"Cool," I said, but the word sounded flat.

"Girls?" Ms. Stone approached us. "Is everything okay?" She was giving us her "why aren't you working" look.

"Yes, Ms. Stone," Mira said. Karly and I nodded.

Okay? I didn't feel okay. I was seriously worried. How was Karly going to prepare for the Quiz Bowl tournament *and* practice for our Holidaze Spectacular routine? I hated that Karly's good news felt like bad news for me.

"Where's Karly?" Ms. Kumar asked me. I looked over at the doorway, hoping she was there, but she wasn't.

"I don't know."

"She's at Quiz Bowl," Kevin said. "Lunchtime practices all this week. And next."

"You'll fill her in?" Ms. Kumar sat on the edge of her desk.

"Yup." Kevin took a bite from his sandwich. Next to him, I unwrapped mine. Karly had Quiz Bowl every day at lunch! Seriously? Well, at least it wouldn't interfere with our evening practices.

"Let's get started." Ms. Kumar set a water bottle down next to her. "We have a lot of ground to cover today, but first I want to say how happy I am that each one of you is here, willing to share your talent with our community. The Holidaze Spectacular is a big event and you all are going to make it a success."

I looked around Ms. Kumar's classroom. There were about thirty of us, all seventh and eighth graders. Most of the kids I knew, or I had seen them perform in school musicals or at recitals. And I'd watched some of the eighth graders in last year's show.

Behind Ms. Kumar on the board was a list of the acts. There were fifteen in all, and at least five of them were in it to win. Of those, I thought our biggest competition was an eighth-grade improv group that came in second last year, and Ryan, an eighth grader who called himself an illusionist. Not a magician—an illusionist. I'd seen him perform last year and, well, he was pretty amazing.

"I want you all to see each other as a team, not as competition." Ms. Kumar took a sip of her water. "I know some of you would like to win the Summer Academy scholarship."

Yes! I looked over at Kevin. He leaned back in his chair and drummed on his chest.

"And that would certainly be a great opportunity, but it is not the main reason we are here. The Holidaze Spectacular is an important fund-raiser for our community. Every year the performers—that's you all—select a community organization or local cause to donate the proceeds from the ticket sales. Does anyone have any ideas?"

"Ms. Kumar?" My hand shot up. "I have an idea."

"Yes, Sasha?"

Then I told the group about the meals program at the Senior Center and how important it was and how it was about to be cut. As I spoke, my voice grew louder and louder. And my face heated up, not because I was embarrassed, but because I cared about Miss Melinda and Big T and everyone else at the Senior Center who counted on the meals.

"This sounds like a very worthy cause. And urgent." Ms. Kumar nodded at me. "Does anyone else have a cause they'd like to support?" No one spoke up, so she continued, "Let's see a show of hands if you want to support the meals program."

Almost everyone in the room raised their hands.

"Excellent. Well, then, that's decided."

Yes! Not only did I have a chance to win the

scholarship, I had a chance to save the meals program. I was going to do everything I could to make
this year's show the most successful one ever!

I leaned forward to focus on what Ms. Kumar was
saying.

"A lot goes on behind the scenes and leading up
to the show. We're going to need volunteers to organize the publicity, decorations, backstage crew,
and refreshments for the reception." Ms. Kumar
looked around the room. "Who would like to volunteer to spearhead the publicity? You'll be in charge
of designing and distributing the flyers, posting on
social media, and other announcements."

"I can do that," I said.

"Great." Ms. Kumar wrote my name down on a pad
of paper. "Thank you."

"Sash," Kevin whispered. "You sure you have
time? It sounds like a lot of work."

I flicked my wrist. "It'll be easy."

Just then Pete Sugarman ran into the classroom.
"Sorry," he mumbled; his eyes dropped down to his
sneakered feet.

"Welcome, Peter," Ms. Kumar said. "Take a seat."

I smiled at him as he made his way to an empty seat in the back row.

"How about decorations?" Ms. Kumar asked. "We're keeping the stage-set simple, but we need decorations for the auditorium. Who would like to organize that?" I looked around the room. Pete opened his brown paper bag. Anna popped a chip in her mouth. No one said anything.

I raised my hand.

"Anyone besides Sasha?" Ms. Kumar scanned the room.

Ryan, who was sitting directly behind me, raised his hand.

"Thank you." She wrote his name on her notepad.

"I'll help too," Kevin said.

"Great." Then she called out the names of the kids who were there but who were not performing in the show. Pete was among them. "You all will be the backstage crew. We need you to help manage the props and keep the show running smoothly."

I looked over at Pete. He nodded at Ms. Kumar.

"Last but certainly not least. We need a volunteer to organize the refreshments. We will be selling these after the show as another way to raise funds for the meals—"

"I'll do it," I called out.

Kevin stared at me.

I turned to face him. *"What?"* I mouthed, but he kept staring. Was he looking at me or past me? I turned around, but only Ryan was there. Kevin must've been staring at me. But why?

"Thank you, Sasha, for your enthusiasm, but you already have a job." Ms. Kumar stepped toward a group of students who were looking at the floor. "I know everyone is worried about practicing for their own act, but this event is about our community. We need everyone to help."

"It's no problem," I said. If I was in charge of the refreshments, I could make sure we had lots to sell and then we'd raise even more money.

"Sasha, last year the refreshment committee baked over a hundred cupcakes. You can't be the only one working on this." Ms. Kumar scanned the group. A few hands shot up and she wrote down the names. "Thank you. Sasha, I'll email you these names and then you can coordinate who makes what. How does that sound?"

"Good."

As Ms. Kumar spoke, Kevin was still looking at me. It was then I thought of my list of clues.

He stares at you. Check.

"I suggest you start a group text so you can coordinate." Ms. Kumar waved her phone in the air. "I know you all are going to make this a great show. Communication and collaboration will be important."

Kevin leaned over toward Ryan and they exchanged phone numbers. Other kids we're doing the same, but for a few seconds I just sat there, feeling good, thinking about how we were going to save the meals program.

Plus, I was doing well on the Kevin front.

So far, Kevin had called me, tried to make me laugh, and stared at me—three out of the six clues. That meant there was a fifty-percent chance he liked me, but that also meant there was a fifty-percent chance—he didn't.

Fifty-fifty—I needed to do better than that.

A lot better.

Chapter Six
GOOD IS NEVER GOOD ENOUGH

After school, Karly waited for me while I talked to Mr. Thomas about the location for the mitten and hat drive tree. He suggested the library, but I wanted the front hall.

"I think that's why the food drive was so successful—because the collection boxes were in the front hall," I explained. "People can't forget about it when it's the first thing they see every day."

Ms. Medley walked into the office then. "Sasha! Just the person I wanted to see. The food bank called earlier to thank us for all the donations. The director was very impressed with you. He said it was the best student-led drive he'd ever seen."

I smiled, then turned toward Mr. Thomas, who sighed.

"Fine," he said. "The front hall it is."

"What's that?" Ms. Medley asked.

"We're going to put the mitten and hat collection in the front hall," I said.

"Excellent," Ms. Medley said. "Excellent."

"How'd it go?" Karly asked as I exited the office.

"Good. Really good." I looked down the hallway. "Where's Kevin?" Usually the three of us walked to JayJay's together.

"He's walking over with Ryan."

"Ryan?"

"Yeah. He's taking acro. He wants to learn some moves for his act."

"But he's an illusionist."

"You've seen him perform. He incorporates all kinds of cool things."

"Great," I said sarcastically. "He was really good before and now he's going to be even better. How are *we* going to win?"

"Sash, we're good too." Karly bumped my dance bag with hers. "And you're really good. Don't worry."

"Karly." I stopped walking. "I am worried. How are we going to stick to our rehearsal schedule with all your Quiz Bowl practices?"

"We'll be fine. Do you honestly think we need to practice twenty hours a week?"

"Okay, maybe my schedule was a little extreme, but no less than fifteen."

"Really Sasha?" Karly groaned.

We sang and danced our way to JayJay's, just like we always did. I no longer felt angry that she hadn't told me about Quiz Bowl. And I wasn't so worried. Fifteen hours a week should be enough.

As we turned onto Main Street, I told Karly about the Holidaze Spectacular meeting and how we were donating the proceeds of the show to the Senior Center's meals program.

"That's a great idea." Karly did a pivot turn on the sidewalk. "You know, Sash. You're really good at this stuff."

"What stuff?" We'd reached JayJay's. In front of us was the floor to ceiling glass window of the studio where the acro class was held.

Karly stopped walking. "Volunteering, organizing. You know, making the world a better place."

Laughing, I dipped into a deep curtsy. "Why thank you." As I straightened, I spotted Kevin inside the studio. Through the glass, I watched as he did a front aerial.

"Wow." I stepped closer. "He's amazing."

"Amazing?" Karly gave me a funny look.

"Yeah." Inside, Kevin's face flushed red. His black hair spiked up (probably from sweat). "He's cute, right?" *Uh oh.* The words came out before I could catch myself.

"No." Karly shook her head. "He's not cute. He's Kevin. And he's being a total show-off." Karly pointed at the glass. On the other side, Kevin and Ryan lunged into walking handstands. Side by side, they moved across the studio.

"You're right," I said. "But *he's* cute." I pointed at Ryan.

"Ryan?" Karly headed toward the entrance. "Sash, you're losing it. I'll tell you who's cute . . . Ahmed."

I swallowed. "How's that going?"

"Not sure, but he told me I was really good at historical facts at practice today."

"He complimented you, that's a good sign."

"You think?"

"Def." Now that I had my own crush (even if it was a total secret) I didn't feel so bad about Karly liking Ahmed.

Sitting on the bench inside JayJay's, Karly and I pulled out our satin ballet shoes. She groaned as she pushed her foot into her pointe shoe and wound the ribbons around her ankles. "This is torture."

"Come on." I bumped her arm with my arm as I tied my ribbons. "It'll get better."

"I don't know. I liked ballet better when we weren't on pointe. Maybe I should quit."

"Quit pointe? But you worked so hard."

"I don't know. I was thinking about dropping the class."

"What? You can't quit!" Karly was a dancer. *We* were dancers. That's what we did.

"Girls, you're late." Ms. Jackson popped her head out of the studio and tapped a nonexistent watch on her wrist.

Ballet class was an hour and fifteen minutes and Ms. Jackson worked us hard. Karly kept falling out of her pirouettes and I struggled to keep my arms in third position arabesque during my grand jeté.

"Focus, girls." Ms. Jackson said. "You're both somewhere else today. Rule number two . . ."

"Be present," Karly and I finished her sentence for her. Rule number one was show up and, at least, we'd both done that.

After dance class, Kevin, Karly, and I walked back to the Hall's house. In their basement, we began choreographing the next section of our routine. At our first rehearsal, we'd decided to start the dance with our backs to the audience. Then we'd turn our heads to the left and then the right. The small movements fit well with the slower music. Then as the music built, our movements would grow bigger. Now we were debating when to turn toward the audience and where to place the knee drop Kevin wanted. Once on the floor, we tried a few moves. We'd done shoulder rolls in a routine at last year's JayJay recital, so we decided to incorporate those. Then Karly and I watched as Kevin showed off a bunch of his acro tricks.

"Enough." Karly put her hands on her hips. "This isn't the Kevin show. If you do all of that, Sasha and I are going to look like your backup dancers."

She was right. "How about you choose two tricks," I said to Kevin.

"Come on." He swatted my arm. "How about three?"

"Fine."

We ran through the opening from the top. When we finished, Kevin and Karly sat down. "It's gonna be great," Karly said.

"I don't know," I said. We were off to a good start, but I was worried the dancing wasn't going to be enough to win. "Do you think we should sing?"

"What are you talking about?" Karly dropped her face into her hands. "We've just spent the last hour choreographing a dance."

"Yeah. One featuring my aerial," Kevin said.

"I mean, what if we could make it even more amazing?"

"How?" Karly lifted her head but she sounded skeptical.

"We could *sing* and dance."

"Seriously?" Kevin raised his eyebrow.

"We all have good voices." I turned toward Karly. "And you have an incredible voice, probably the best at school. Think how much more we'll impress the judge if we dance *and* sing." I wiggled my fingers.

"This is for the Summer Academy, for the High School for Performing Arts. The expectations are going to be high. We need to—"

"Fine," Karly said. "We'll give it a try."

"Is good ever good enough for you?" Kevin stuck his tongue out at me and rolled his eyes.

We ran through the opening. But this time we turned the music low and sang.

"Uh, cringe." Karly turned off the music. "That was terrible."

The truth was, Karly sounded great. Kevin and me? Not so good. "We just need more practice. What do you think?" I asked as Karly and Kevin dropped to the ground, breathing hard. "Are you willing to do the work?"

"Sure," Kevin said.

"Sash, sometimes I seriously wish you weren't such an overachiever." Karly wiped a strand of hair out of her eyes.

"But admit it, you think it's a better act, don't you?"

"It's a lot harder."

"Dinner!" Mr. Hall called down to us.

"But harder is better—more impressive," I said.

"We can do this." Kevin bounded toward the stairs. "But right now, I need food."

"I should probably get going," I said, but I didn't want to. As I neared the top step, their dinner smelled good. Really good.

"Sasha, your mom says you can stay." Mrs. Hall smiled, putting her phone on the counter. "It's your favorite."

"Lasagna?"

"Yup. And garlic bread."

"Yum. Thanks!" I loved eating dinner at the Hall's house and I loved that Mrs. Hall knew I loved lasagna.

At dinner, we talked all about the show and how we were raising money for the meals program at the Senior Center.

"What an excellent idea," Mr. Hall said.

"It was Sasha's," Kevin said and then he turned toward me. "What was up with you at the meeting today? You volunteered for everything." He popped a green bean into his mouth.

"That's great." Mrs. Hall handed Kevin a napkin. "Nothing gets done without volunteers." She stood up. "Anyone want seconds?"

"No, thank you," I said. "Everything was delicious."

"Sash, you better start baking now." Kevin wiped his mouth with the napkin. "How many cupcakes do you need to make? A thousand?"

"Ha, ha." I stood up to clear my plate. "I think we'll make cookies this year."

"Better make two thousand then."

"Kevin. Stop teasing Sasha," Mr. Hall said as he followed me into the kitchen.

He teases you. That was on my list of clues! Check.

"That's okay," I said. "I don't mind." And I didn't. Because I'd reached a sixty-six percent chance that Kevin liked me. True, if I got a sixty-six on a test, I'd still be upset, but I was headed in the right direction.

After dinner, Mom picked me up.

"How was your day?" she asked as I slid into the front seat of the car.

But before I could answer, Mom had moved on. "Did you go to the Robotics meeting at lunch today?"

"No. Why?"

"Did I forget to tell you? I read about it in the school newsletter. They meet on Mondays and are looking for new members."

"Mom, I have meetings for the show on Mondays."

"But that will end in a few weeks. You should go talk to the Robotics advisor and ask if you can join in January."

I said nothing as I popped in my earbuds and played "Winter Dreams." I closed my eyes. Listening to the music, I ran through the opening of our routine. I pictured my arms rising, my feet flexing, my body turning. I pushed away Mom's nagging and I escaped to my happy place where only music and movement flowed.

chapter seven
RED, WHITE, AND GLUE

On Saturday, I waited for Karly in the lobby of the Senior Center. When she didn't show up I texted her:

WHERE R U?

When she didn't respond, I headed to the dining room, but I was feeling salty and I kept checking my phone. After Monday, she'd arrived late to all our rehearsals and she'd even skipped dance class at JayJay's on Wednesday. I'd been right to worry about Karly making the Holidaze Spectacular a priority. Because she wasn't.

"Where's Karly?" Miss Melinda asked when she spotted me.

"I don't know."

"Must be a boy." Miss Melinda sat down at her usual table.

Yeah. Probably. Whenever I did see Karly, that's all she talked about. *Ahmed this, Ahmed that* and then *Quiz Bowl this, Quiz Bowl that.*

"Would you like some Jell-O?" I asked, eyeing the small bowls of wiggling green on a nearby tray.

"Yes, please." Miss Melinda touched my arm. "Thank you."

Later when I brought applesauce over to Big T, he also asked me about Karly.

"Sorry," I said. "She's not here today."

"Oh no. She promised to show me how to do a high kick."

"She did?"

He laughed.

Then the director came over and gave me a hug. "Sasha, I spoke with Ms. Kumar and she told me the news. Thank you!" And for a moment I forgot about being mad at Karly.

As I was leaving the Senior Center, Pete Sugarman was coming in, carrying a tray filled with Mr. Sugarman's fresh-baked cookies. Smiling, I held the door open for him.

"Thanks," he said, and smiled back.

I unzipped my coat as I headed down the front steps to Mom's car. The plan was to swing by the Hall's house to pick up Kevin and then go shopping for the materials we needed to make our costumes, but with Karly not showing up at the Senior Center, we needed to pick her up too.

But when only Kevin came out of the house, my anger tightened. *Where was she?*

Kevin jumped off the front steps and did a pivot turn at the curb.

"Now, that's what I call an entrance," Mom said as Kevin opened the car door.

"Where's Karly?" I tried to sound calm but I was ready for a full-blown freak-out.

"Emergency Quiz Bowl practice."

"Seriously?"

"She says she'll be back in time for us to rehearse."

"But she has our shopping list."

"Ta-da!" Kevin pulled a slip of paper from his coat pocket and handed it to me.

I read it: tulle, white tights and leotards, fabric paint, a morph suit for Kevin, and mini candy cane appliqués.

"Where to first?" Mom asked. "The dance store?"

"Sounds good." Kevin buckled his seat belt and looked over at me. "What's the problem, Sash? You don't think I'm as good a shopper as Karly?" He stuck up his nose. "Well, I'm going to show you."

As I laughed, my anger over Karly loosened. Kevin and I always had fun together. Plus, now I could use the time to figure out if he *like* liked me. I still had two more clues to check off.

At DanceXtreme, Mom stayed in the front of the store while Kevin and I walked toward the back. Kevin, Karly, and I had pooled together our birthday and babysitting money. We had a budget of sixty dollars. That wasn't much for what we needed.

"Let's head to the clearance aisle," I said, touching a gold lamé leotard as I passed by the New Arrivals rack.

"Whoa!" Kevin stopped. "This is awesome!" He pulled out the hanger and held out the shimmery leotard. "I should wear this, don't you think?"

"Ha, ha," I said, swiping it from him and placing it back on the rack. "Come on."

It turned out Kevin was a pretty decent shopper. He found the discounted white leotards for Karly and me. Granted they had a pumpkin embroidered below the neckline, but we were pretty sure we could sew a candy cane patch over that and no one would know. We bought Kevin a red morph suit on sale, too. And we had a buy-one-get-one-free coupon for tights.

At the checkout, I popped a rhinestone tiara on my head.

"What do you think?" I tilted my head toward Kevin.

He gave me a quick glance and said, "Gorge!" Then he turned back to the employee who was getting a price check on the morph suit.

Gorge? Had Kevin just called me gorgeous? Did that count for the *He compliments you* clue?

Uh . . . yeah, technically. But he barely looked at me when he said it, and well, the word—gorge (was it even a word?)—was kind of over the top. I decided I'd hold out for a more sincere compliment.

In the car, Mom let us blast the music. She even belted out the "Winter Dreams" refrain. Kevin and I were actually starting to sound pretty good. By the time we arrived at the fabric and craft store, I'd forgotten about being angry with Karly.

Inside the store, we passed a bin of feathery, hot pink boas. Kevin grabbed one and put it on.

"What do you think?" He flipped the ends of it over his shoulder and ran his fingers through his hair.

"Gorge," I said and then laughed.

A Christmas song blasted from the store speaker.

"Let's dance!" Kevin sashayed down the fabric aisle. Laughing, I followed.

"What do you think?" I pulled out a bolt of red polka-dot tulle, but Kevin wasn't paying attention. "Kev?"

"Yeah." He stared down the paint aisle.

"Focus." I shoved the fabric in front of him. "Do you like this or the shimmery one?"

"Is that Ryan?" Kevin asked.

"Where?" I put down the bolt. There was Ryan wearing a top hat and a long black cape, standing in front of a display of brushes. "Yep."

"Hey, Ryan!" Kevin headed toward him. "Nice costume."

I followed, leaving the bolts of tulle out on the table behind us.

"What's up?" Ryan fist bumped Kevin, and then looked at me. "You guys shopping for the show?"

"Yup. Costumes," Kevin said. "How 'bout you?"

"Props for my act."

"I know what you should do." Kevin grabbed a jar of purple paint from the shelf. "Change the color of the auditorium from puke green to grape."

Ryan laughed. "If only."

"Are you going to do the cell phone trick this year?" I asked. At last year's show, Ryan's finale was getting a bunch of the cell phones in the audience to start ringing at the same time. And they weren't just ringing—their ringtones played a song. No one could figure out how he did it.

"I'm working on something new." He looked over at Kevin. "And I want to show off some of my acro moves in between tricks."

Hearing Ryan talk about his act made me feel worried about ours.

"You should definitely add a fish flop." Kevin dropped to the floor and did one. But with his puffy coat on he looked like an oversized flounder.

Again, Ryan laughed.

"Kev." I rolled my eyes. "Get up."

"What, Sasha?" Kevin jumped up, brushing off his jeans. "I thought you'd be impressed."

Impressed? My mind jumped to the final clue on

my checklist: *He tries to impress you.* Was Kevin trying to impress me with his fish flop? Or was he being
sarcastic?

Mmm . . . sarcastic.

"Come on." I pulled Kevin back toward the fabric.
"We need to decide on how much tulle for the tutus."

"Tulle? Tutus?" Ryan said. "Now I'm really afraid
to compete against you guys."

"Oh, shut up." Then I lifted my hand in a single
wave and headed toward the fabric. Kevin trailed
behind.

"What do you think? Five feet? Six?" I held out a
swatch of the shimmery tulle, but Kevin wasn't listening. He was staring back at the paint aisle.

"You think he's going to win, don't you?"

"What?" Kevin turned around like he had no idea
what I was talking about.

"You think Ryan's going to win?"

Kevin shrugged. "I don't know."

"He's not. We are." I paused. "Now come on. We
need to make a decision about the tulle."

"How'd it go?" Karly asked as Kevin and I walked
through the front door of the Hall's house. I didn't

say anything to her. I hung up my coat and laid out our haul on the kitchen table without even looking at her.

"Sasha, come on," Karly said. "Don't be mad."

"You didn't show up at the Senior Center this morning." I turned toward her.

"I forgot."

"Didn't you get my text?"

"I did. But by then it was too late. And I didn't want you to be mad."

"I *am* mad. And then you blew off shopping after you promised you could do it."

"Sash, the Quiz Bowl tournament is in two weeks."

"Yeah, and the Holidaze Spectacular is soon too."

Karly stepped toward the table and picked up the red morph suit. "Nice," she said, but I could see she was eyeing the pumpkins on the leotards.

"They were on sale," I explained.

Kevin dropped a large candy cane appliqué down on the leotard. It covered the pumpkin.

"See," I said.

"We're going to sew these on, and once Dad makes the tutus, we'll add these." Kevin dumped out a package of smaller candy cane appliqués. "And these."

He pointed to a jar of quarter-sized sequins. "It'll be great." He pushed Karly and me toward each other. "Can you two make up already? We need to practice."

"Fine," I said.

Karly gave me a half hug and then we headed down the stairs to the basement. When I stepped inside the studio, the first thing I noticed was the yellow sticky notes. There must've been a hundred of them covering the mirror.

"What happened down here?" I asked. "A Post-it note explosion?"

"Quiz Bowl prep," Karly said.

"Down here?" I peeled a sticky note off the mirror and glanced down at Karly's neat handwriting. "Really?" How were we going to see what we were doing?

"Yeah. That way I can practice for Quiz Bowl while we dance." She nodded toward the sticky note in my hand. "Test me."

I looked down at the question and read, "What does a herpetologist study?"

"Snakes and lizards."

I flipped over the sticky note. "Right." I handed it to Karly. "Now we need to focus on singing and dancing. We still need to choreograph the ending."

Kevin started singing "Winter Dreams" in a ridiculously high voice.

"And you need to give Kevin some voice lessons."

Karly laughed, and in that moment, I felt like everything might be okay.

Using the barre, the three of us stretched, and then Karly led us in some vocal warm-up exercises. Without dancing, we ran through the song a couple of times and we were actually starting to sound pretty good. Then we choreographed the next section. Kevin wanted to add a triple cartwheel. Karly didn't want to try, but I did. So Kevin and I practiced, but my feet kept hitting him in the face as I turned.

"Almost," Kevin said as I finished the third rotation.

"How'd it look?" I asked Karly, who was sitting on the floor, a sticky note in her hand.

"Great." She turned the note over and looked at the backside.

"You weren't even watching," I said.

"What?" Karly pulled another sticky note off the mirror.

"Time for a break," Kevin said.

Upstairs, Mr. Hall was sitting at the sewing

machine in the family room. I had total faith in his creative abilities. For Halloween, he'd made our pirate costumes and we'd won an honorable mention at the town parade. Which was excellent, considering we were up against adorable babies dressed as ladybugs.

"Ta-da." He lifted up a tutu made from the tulle. "Now's the fun part. Decorating them. Do you want to hand stitch the appliqués and the sequins on or use a glue gun?"

"Glue gun," Kevin said. "Of course."

Karly rolled her eyes. "Just don't glue your fingers together again."

"That was superglue."

"Whatever," Karly said as we sat down at the table. Mr. Hall handed her a tutu. "These are going to be cute."

I held a felt candy cane in my hand. "Super cute."

"Sash, would you mind quizzing me while we worked?" Karly handed me a stack of sticky notes.

"Seriously?"

"Please."

Looking down at the top sticky note, I sighed.

"Fine. What's the largest two digit prime number less than 100?"

Chapter Eight
CHEERS!

"Are you sure you don't want to come to the library?" Mom asked as she parked the car in front of Sugarman's. It was Sunday afternoon. "They're offering a STEM workshop later." She looked over at me. "And we can sign you up for the coding course, the one I told you about. It starts in January."

"I can't. Mira's meeting me here. I promised I'd help her revise her social studies essay." I opened the car door.

Mom touched the sleeve of my coat. "The workshop starts at 3:30, in case you change your mind."

"Mom."

"Fine. We'll talk about it later."

"There's nothing to talk about." I got out of the car.

"I'll see you at home," Mom said as I shut the door.

I doubted if the apartment was ever going to feel like home to me. Not the way our old house did—filled with memories of all of us being a family. I hated the three-hour time difference to California and Dad and Claire. Every time I called or texted Claire, it seemed like it was a bad time. Last night, I wanted to talk to her about Kevin and how there was a good chance he liked me, but when I called she was just getting out of the shower; the time before that she was heading to a party. How was I ever going to get the advice I needed when there was never a good time to talk?

Inside Sugarman's, I took a seat in the back at the table pushed up against the wall. I smelled the fresh batch of cookies, ground coffee, and cocoa.

"How about a sample?" Mr. Sugarman stood in front of me with a plate of chocolate chip cookies.

"Thanks a lot!" I bit into the gooey sweetness.

"Sasha!" Mira called from the front of the store.

Mr. Sugarman looked at my laptop as I pulled it out of my backpack. "I'm thinking about getting Pete one of those for Hanukkah."

I stopped chewing and swallowed. "A laptop? That's a great gift. Mine was Claire's, so it's older, but it's still good." I pointed out the brand on the back of my screen. That was when I noticed one of Karly's Quiz Bowl yellow sticky notes stuck to it. *How did that get there?* I wondered as I peeled it off and put it in my binder to give to her later.

Mira sat down in the seat across from me. "Hi, Mr. Sugarman."

"Can I get you girls something to drink? How about a gingerbread mocha? Or a hot cocoa with extra whip?"

"Yes, please," Mira said. "I'd like a hot cocoa."

After yesterday's costume buying, I was a little low on funds, but I wanted something too. "May I have the peppermint cocoa, please?"

"Sure. One Candy Cane Cocoa coming up."

"Let me pull up your essay," I said to Mira as she leaned over to face my screen. But I clicked on the wrong document.

"What's this?" Mira asked as she started to read. "The Clues: He calls or texts you. He tries to make you laugh—"

"It's nothing!" I tried to close the computer but Mira pushed my hand away and kept reading.

"He stares at you. He teases you. He compliments you. He tries to impress you."

Mortified, I hit the key to close it.

"Sash, did you really create a Google doc to try to figure out if your crush likes you?" Mira leaned back in her chair, smiling widely. "You're such a geek."

"Gee, thanks."

"I mean it in a good way." She put her elbows on the table. "So come on, you can tell me. Who do you like?"

Just then Pete came over with our drinks. I hoped he hadn't heard what we were talking about.

"Here you go," he said, putting a mug in front of me. I caught a whiff of peppermint.

"Thank you." I looked up at him. My face felt very warm. It must've been the steam from the drink.

"You're welcome." He smiled.

I leaned over and blew on my cocoa to cool it down, watching as Pete disappeared on the other side of the counter.

"Cheers!" Mira raised up her mug. I picked up mine and we clinked our drinks together. "To crushes and to you helping me fix my social studies essay."

"Let's see it." I put down my drink and opened up Mira's essay. As soon as I started reading, I knew

Mira had a lot of work to do. "Did you print out a copy? It'll be easier to edit."

Mira dug through her backpack. "Here." She pulled out a crumpled piece of paper and handed it to me.

I pressed it against the table, trying to smooth out the wrinkles. In my other hand I lifted up my red flair marker.

"Be nice," she said, as I underlined a run-on sentence, and then circled a misspelled word, and then another.

A few minutes later, I handed her back the essay.

"Ouch! Did I do anything right?" Mira said as she looked at the red marks all over her paper.

"Your last sentence is strong, but you need to rework your introduction and you're missing supporting evidence in the second paragraph."

"Anything else?" Mira tilted her head back as she took her last sip of the cocoa.

"Spell-check is your friend."

She sighed. "I'm going to the library." She put the mug down on the table. "It'll be easier for me to work there. You wanna come?"

"No thanks." I was not interested in running into Mom and being forced to sign my life away to learn how to code. "I was kind of hoping you'd help me with the flyer for the show. Ms. Kumar wants me to show her something by tomorrow."

"Sorry, Sash." She slipped her arms into her coat. "Thanks to you, this essay is going to take me forever."

"Good luck," I called as she headed down the cereal aisle to the door. I'd handed in my essay early, so I had plenty of time to work on the flyer. But I wanted the flyer to be perfect. The more tickets we sold, the more money we raised for the Senior Center.

I opened up my computer and stared at the blank page.

When my phone pinged, I picked it up. It was a text from Kevin, asking me what time acro was. Why was Kevin texting *me* about that? There was a special acro dance workshop that afternoon at JayJay's with a big-time dancer from New York City, but Kevin knew I wasn't going. The workshop cost seventy-five dollars . . . so even if I was into acro, it would've been too expensive.

Me: *idk*

Kevin: *Huh?*

Me: *I'm not going. Remember?*

Kevin: *Sorry. Texident!*

Texident—Kevin claimed he made up the word. I'm sure he didn't, but considering how many times he'd sent me a text thinking I was Karly, he should have. I wondered who he thought he was texting. It definitely wasn't Karly. It must've been someone in his acro dance class. I sent him a smiley face emoji and put down my phone.

I started on the flyer, but nothing I did looked good. All the clip art seemed too basic and the fonts I chose just seemed wrong. After about twenty minutes when I'd deleted the same three lines about five times, I took a break and headed to the bathroom.

On the way back to the table, I passed Pete posting a flyer on the Market's Community Bulletin Board.

"Hey," I said.

"Hi." A thumbtack dropped out of his hand.

I picked it up and pushed the tack into the corner of the colorful flyer Pete was hanging.

"Thanks."

"Downtown D'Lights," I read the words off the flyer. "I forgot that was coming up." D'Lights was an annual event organized by the Main Street store owners to promote downtown holiday shopping. It was a night when shops stayed open late, giving away candy and door prizes, and there were a bunch of free activities. The downtown businesses went all out with decorations, especially with light displays.

"Yeah. It's this Saturday. We're setting up a hot chocolate stand by the ice skating rink," Pete said. "It'll be between the tree and the menorah."

"Nice," I said, staring at the flyer, which looked like it had been hand-drawn. "That's really artistic." I pointed to the lettering. Holiday lights were drawn to look like they were hanging off each word.

"You think?"

I nodded. "I wish I could come up with something like that for the Holidaze Spectacular." I pulled out my phone and took a picture of the flyer.

"What are you doing?" Pete asked.

"Posting it to Instagram," I said as I headed back to the table.

Within seconds, I had twenty likes and a string of comments. The first one was from Kevin: *Be there*.

Did that mean something? I opened up my Google doc and read the final two clues.

He compliments you.

He tries to impress you.

"Did you finish your social studies essay?" Pete's voice startled me. I looked up. He was sitting at the table next to mine, drawing on a piece of butcher-block paper spread in front of him.

"Yeah."

"Me too." He set down his pen. "What're you working on now?"

"Uh . . ." I closed the Google doc and opened up the blank document. "The Holidaze Spectacular flyer. I told Ms. Kumar I'd have something by tomorrow, but I'm having trouble coming up with ideas."

"You want help?"

"Sure!" As Pete walked toward me, I smiled, noticing the toes of his sneakers were again covered in what looked like powdered sugar.

Pete sat down next to me. "Let's see what you have so far."

I pointed to the computer.

"Well." He looked at the blank screen. "You've got to start somewhere. I've got an idea." He went over and grabbed his pen and a section of the butcher-block paper, and started sketching a stage with curtains. "We could put the wording here." He pointed to space between the curtains. "Add a string of lights. What do you think?"

"I think you're a really good artist." I was impressed—who knew Pete was so talented? I glanced back over at the Community Bulletin Board. "You did the flyer for Dowtown D'Lights, didn't you?"

"Yeah." Pete smiled.

Just then my stomach felt funny—fluttery, kind of queasy. But I ignored it and focused on the flyer. Mostly I tossed out ideas and Pete drew them, showing me what they would look like. Before I knew it, Mom called to tell me it was time for dinner.

"I'll work on it some more, "Pete said. "Then I'll bring it to the meeting tomorrow. Okay?"

"That would be amazing." I stood up.

Smiling wide, Pete stood up too. "Good."

"Thanks," I said, feeling a little dizzy. I hoped I wasn't coming down with something. I definitely didn't have time to get sick. I had way too much to do.

Outside Sugarman's, I popped in my earbuds and put "Winter Dreams" on repeat. With the fresh air on my face, I sang and danced all the way home, feeling great.

Chapter Nine
THE HAT

I arrived at school early on Monday morning to set up for the mitten and hat drive. First, I hung up the poster I'd made for it. (I probably could've used Pete's artistic skills, but it was fine. Actually, my red and white bubble letters looked pretty good.) Then I started to set up the artificial tree—Mr. Thomas had left the box in the hall for me. As I pulled out the top section of branches, a gust of cold air hit my back.

"You need help?" It was Ryan. Before I could answer, he dropped his backpack next to mine.

"Thanks," I said as we lifted it up together and secured it into place. The tree was very pink. Very neon.

"What's it for?" Ryan stood back, taking off his hat and stuffing it in his pocket.

I pointed to my poster on the wall. "You want to donate?" More kids entered the school, more blasts of cold air.

"Sure." Ryan picked up his backpack. "And you should talk to the Knitting Club—maybe they could make stuff."

"That's a good idea!"

"Nice tree!" Kevin stood behind us, unzipping his coat.

"What's up?" Ryan fist bumped Kevin.

I straightened a bent branch and then stepped back; the bare tree looked a little sad. "I hope we can fill it."

"You've got this, Sash." Kevin smiled. "Think about what you did with the food drive. You're good at this."

I stepped forward to fix another branch. Had Kevin just complimented me? Uh . . . yes!

"Kev?" I wanted to ask him about his social studies essay (and make sure he'd finished it), but when I turned back, Kevin and Ryan were already gone—halfway down the hallway. "Wait up!" I called, swinging my backpack onto my shoulder. As I ran to catch up, I was thinking about the crush checklist.

He compliments you. Check. Only one clue left and then I would know if Kevin liked me for sure.

"We need to step up the publicity." Ms. Kumar stood in front of her desk at our Monday lunch meeting for the Holidaze Spectacular. "The town paper has been running a Save the Date ad for a few weeks, but now's the time to promote on social media. Pete and Sasha made an excellent flyer."

"It was really Pete," I said as Kevin patted my shoulder and whispered, "Great job." Then he picked up his sandwich and took a big bite.

Ms. Kumar continued, "Sasha and Pete, you'll be in charge of making copies." She nodded at us. "But the rest of you will need to help distribute them."

"I'll help," Kevin mumbled, his mouth full of food.

"I have good news," Ms. Kumar said. "The auditorium is available for you all to practice during lunch this week and next." She lifted up a clipboard. "Sign-ups will be here." She put the clipboard on her desk. A couple of kids in the front row lurched forward to sign up right then, but Ms. Kumar told them they needed to wait until she finished.

I slumped in my seat. There was no point to Kevin and me signing up, not with Karly at Quiz Bowl practice every day at lunch. It burned me that all the other acts were going to have the advantage of practicing on the stage while we wouldn't have the chance until the dress rehearsal. Thank you, Karly.

Then Ms. Kumar led us to the auditorium. Someone from the school yearbook was meeting us there to take a photograph. In the hall, I walked next to Kevin, but he was laughing with Ryan about something that happened at the acro dance workshop the day before, so it was hard to get his attention.

"Are you okay with the flyer?" Pete walked on the other side of me. "I made a few changes."

"It looks great!" I said. It really did. "Hey, I had another idea for publicity. I was thinking of making a short video, like a commercial. We could put it online. Ms. Kumar said it was a good idea. Want to help?"

"Sure," Pete said.

"Okay, cool." My stomach felt jittery. I knew I shouldn't have had that soda.

Once inside the auditorium, we all posed while the photographer snapped a few shots. I sat in the front with my legs hanging over the edge of the stage.

"Awesome!" Kevin said from behind me. Turning around, I saw him pop a shiny black top hat on his head.

Where did he get that? It was ridiculous looking—too big, too shiny, too much like something a middle-aged magician would wear at a little kid's birthday party.

When Ms. Kumar dismissed us, I stood up and walked over to Kevin, pointing at the hat.

"Awesome, huh?" He tugged on the brim. "It'll look great with the morph suit."

"Uh, no."

"No? What do you mean—no?"

"You're *not* wearing that for our performance."

"Come on, Sash." He turned his head from side to side, posing. "You love it, right?"

"Definitely not. Where'd you get it?"

Kevin glanced over at Ryan, who had just jumped off the stage. "Hey, Ryan!"

Ryan swiveled back around.

"Thanks!" Kevin called, tapping the top of the hat.

"I know why he gave it to you," I said as I watched Ryan leave the auditorium. "He wants to win. The judge from the Summer Academy won't take us seriously if you wear that ridiculous hat. She'll be so distracted by it, she won't even see our performance."

"I think it's just what we need." Kevin ran his hand along the brim. "It's classic."

"Classic? Remember our theme? Candy canes?"

"We could add a few of the appliqués." He touched the sides.

"To the hat?" I pulled it off his head. "Never," I said, hiding it behind my back. Kevin lurched forward, trying to grab it back.

We were both laughing hard, but there was no way I was going to let him wear that hat. When the drama teacher walked in, Kevin stopped. Then, with the hat in my hand, I jumped off the stage.

"See ya!" I called, waving the top hat as I ran out of the auditorium.

After ballet class at JayJay's, Karly and I sat on the bench outside the studio. We were waiting for Kevin to finish his class.

"You know, everyone else in the show is getting

stage time to rehearse during lunch." I lifted up my water bottle and took a sip.

"I know." Karly stared into the ballet studio in front of us where a class of tutu-wearing preschoolers wobbled as they pliéed. "I'm sorry."

"Sorry? That's all you can say?"

"Sash, I know it sucks, but I really care about Quiz Bowl. And the tournament is in eleven days."

"You've told me."

Karly nodded, but she didn't say anything.

"Did you see the hat Kevin wants to wear for our routine?" I took another drink of water.

"Yeah." Karly untied the ribbons on her pointe shoes. Stretching out her legs, she flexed her feet. "I take it the hat is not Sasha-approved."

"Definitely not. But don't worry. I'm keeping it away from him until after the show."

"I kind of liked it!"

"What? Are you kidding me?" I grabbed my sweat-shirt from my bag.

"I don't know. I thought it was . . . fresh."

"Seriously?" I put on my sweatshirt. "Fresh?"

"Fresh?" Kevin approached. "You two want to see something fresh?"

"Sure." Karly rolled her eyes as she stood up.

Kevin looked directly at me. "Get ready to be impressed."

I smiled as Karly and I followed Kevin into the acro dance studio.

"Hey," Ryan waved, his back to us. He faced the mirror.

"You ready?" Kevin asked; Ryan nodded.

Karly and I watched as the two of them did a bunch of stunts. They finished with coordinated front walkovers.

Karly and I clapped as they bowed.

"Impressive," I said.

"I'm glad you liked it." Kevin winked, then made a goofy face.

Ryan said something about the acro workshop they went to the day before, but I wasn't listening, I was thinking how Kevin had wanted to impress me.

He tries to impress you. Check.

YES!

It was true—one hundred percent certain: Kevin liked me. I felt then like I did when I aced a test or when I saw my name listed on the High Honor Roll. I had set a goal, and I had achieved it.

"Ms. Jackson said studio four is available. We can practice our routine there." Karly tilted her head toward the door. "The sooner we get this done, the sooner I can study."

"You're killin' me with all this Quiz Bowl prep." Kevin reached down for his dance bag where one of Karly's sticky notes was stuck to the side. He pulled it off and stuck it to his forehead. "Maybe if you attach them directly to your brain, you won't have to study."

Karly snatched the sticky note off his head. "Come on." She tugged my arm as I stifled a laugh.

"I'll be right there," Kevin said as Karly and I left the studio.

As we walked, she looked down and I knew she was reading the sticky note.

"What's the question?" I asked.

"Where's the Daniel Boone National Forest?" She crumpled the sticky note and threw it into the nearby trash can.

"Eastern Kentucky," we both said at the exact same time.

"Sasha?" Karly raised her eyebrow. "You sure you don't want to join the team?"

"I'm sure." I headed over to the water fountain.

"You know . . . it's been fun hanging out with Ahmed," Karly said as I bent over to refill my water bottle. "I really like him. I mean, whenever I'm near him, my knees even feel all weak and wobbly!"

"Really?" My knees had never felt anything when I stood next to Kevin. I tightened the cap on my water bottle. "Is that even a thing? I mean, it sounds so Hollywood."

"Of course it's a thing. Anyway, I think he feels the same way, but I'm not totally sure."

I didn't say anything. I was thinking about how it was nice to know Kevin liked me (for sure). Would we become a couple (whatever that meant) soon? I was determined to make Sash-evin a thing. No, maybe not Sashevin . . . Kev-asha. Yes. I liked the sound of that.

I just needed to figure out how.

Chapter Ten
THE NEXT STEP

"He likes me," I said to Claire on the phone in my room with the door closed. (I did *not* need Mom in on this conversation.) "I'm sure of it!" With my free hand, I pulled the top hat—the one Ryan had given to Kevin—out of my dance bag where I'd stashed it.

"Did he tell you he likes you?" Claire sounded rushed, but it was Monday night, and I knew she wouldn't be headed to a party.

I tossed the hat into the air and caught it. "No, not exactly, but he does all the things a boy does when he likes you."

"Well, that's great." Claire said. "Who's your crush again?"

"Kevin." I dropped the hat onto the top of my bookshelf. "I told you that. Like twice."

"Oh. Kevin?" She paused. "Really?"

"Yes. Kevin. Really." I glanced down at my computer where I'd saved a photo of the High School for Performing Arts building as my screen saver. "So what do I do now? Do I tell him?"

"Sash, I'm sorry, I've got to go. Elena and I are headed to the dining hall."

"Now? But it's nine o'clock at night?"

"There, it's nine. Here, it's six o'clock. And I need to eat dinner."

Fine.

Without Claire's help, I did the next best thing. I Googled: "How do I tell a boy I like him?" Then I started scrolling through some of the sites. The advice was all pretty basic—tell him in person, get someone else to tell him for you, text him, or give him a note.

I wasn't going to get one of our friends to tell him. That seemed too embarrassing. Texting felt weird, and a note seemed totally awkward.

I imagined standing in front of Kevin and telling him. The website said to make eye contact, touch his arm, smile, and don't rush. I felt ridiculous just thinking about it. No—that wasn't going to work. I kept searching, trying to find something that seemed like a good idea. And then . . . *bam*. There it was!

Invite him to do something with you. I found it in an article called "What to Do When You're Afraid to Tell Someone You Like Them."

I could do that. But what should I ask him to do?

Before I said good night to my phone (Mom made me keep it on the kitchen counter when I went to bed), I scrolled through Instagram, tapping on a bunch of photos, including ones of Kevin and Ryan doing acro tricks. There was one photo I stared at for a long time but I didn't heart it. It was of Karly and Ahmed sitting together at Sugarman's. When was that taken? Were they on some sort of date? Finally, I scrolled past it. My last post was the picture of the Downtown D'Lights flyer. Over two hundred people liked it. I reread Kevin's comment: *Be there.*

That was when I decided my next step. I'd ask Kevin to go with me to D'Lights Night. It wasn't the kind of thing you needed a date for at all—older kids hung out in groups and younger kids went with their families (before the divorce, we'd always gone as a family). But I thought about the twinkling lights and the smell of hot cocoa, and it seemed perfect. Perfectly romantic. I typed a text to Kevin: *U want 2 go 2 D'Lights Night?* When I reread the words, I knew something was missing. So I added: *with me.*

Me: *U want 2 go 2 D'Lights Night with me?*

I waited and then the dots appeared . . . the three little dots . . . dot, dot, dotting on my screen. I held my breath, waiting.

And then, *ping.*

Kevin: *Y*

Yesssss! From the top of my bookshelf, I picked up the silly top hat and spun it on my hand. Yesssss! Kevin and I were going to Downtown D'Lights on Saturday night. Together. It would be a date. A first date! Everything was coming together. Karly might have Ahmed, but I had Kevin (almost, sort of). I was excited and nervous, like I was about to take a big test I'd studied hard for.

In the cafeteria on Tuesday, I made my way through the line, wishing I'd packed my lunch. The fish sticks smelled too fishy. The peas looked mushy. The bread roll was rock hard. But when I saw Karly grab a bottle of chocolate milk from the bin, my mood lifted.

"You eating down here?" I asked, hoping she was.

"No." She grabbed another milk and an apple juice. "Quiz Bowl. We're meeting in Mrs. Giberga's room today."

"Oh." I looked down at my tray; the peas rolled into a fish stick.

"See ya!" she called, but I didn't respond. I was trying to figure out where I was going to sit. Scanning the tables, I looked for Kevin. He was the only one in our group who wouldn't be in the auditorium practicing. Someone bumped me; my unopened milk carton toppled onto the fish stick covered with peas. I needed to sit down, but where? When I saw a spot next to a girl in my science class, I headed over to her table, but as I reached it another girl slid into the seat. Carrying my tray, I walked around the cafeteria, desperate to find a seat and wondering where Kevin was. Finally, I saw an open spot at a table of eighth graders. I didn't know any of them, and I hoped they wouldn't tell me I couldn't sit there.

"Hey," a girl said to me as I sat down, and then she

resumed her conversation about a basketball game with her friend sitting across from her.

"Hey," I mumbled, feeling pretty awkward, but at least I had a seat.

It turned out the whole table was on the girls' basketball team. When they described the set-up for the winning point in their last game, I sat silently running through our dance routine. We still hadn't choreographed the ending. I was thinking we might want to add a lift (Kevin lifting me), but at our last practice, Karly had said she didn't think we were ready for that.

Where was Kevin? I knew Mira and Anna were in the auditorium rehearsing, but Kevin should've been in the cafeteria. As I chewed a piece of rubbery fish stick, I looked around the loud cafeteria. But I couldn't find him. Which just made me feel more alone.

"Sasha!" I looked up, and there was Pete walking toward me.

"Hey Pete!" I felt better already.

"Ms. Kumar wants us to make copies of the flyer." He waved a paper in his hand.

"Let's do it!" I was psyched to escape the cafeteria.

Pete walked with me as I threw away my trash and set my tray on the rack. Then we headed to the office. We didn't talk, but unlike sitting at the table with the girls' basketball team, I didn't feel awkward. When we arrived at the copier, the front panel was open, and Ahmed knelt on the ground peering inside the machine.

"What's up?" I asked.

"I was making copies for our practice round when the machine just stopped." He hit the side panel and glanced up at the clock on the wall.

"Don't hit it." I stepped forward. "Let me look."

Ahmed and I traded places. I had made a lot of copies for the Food Drive and other community service activities, so I knew the machine. I opened up another panel and pulled out a half-crumpled sheet of paper. Then I closed everything, gently pressing the main panel shut.

"It was a paper jam." I stood up and pressed the restart button. The machine hummed. "It'll work now."

"Thanks," Ahmed said.

Pete looked over at me and smiled.

I smiled back, and felt my face heat up. Did Pete think I was a nerd for knowing so much about the copier? Taking the elastic off my wrist, I pulled my hair into a ponytail, which made my neck feel cooler.

Karly walked into the office. "What's taking so long?" she asked Ahmed, and then noticed Pete and me. "Oh, hey! What's up?"

"Not much. We're just waiting to make copies for the Holidaze Spectacular flyer," I said.

"I'm done." Ahmed picked up a stack of papers.

"Cool," Karly said, but I wasn't sure if she was talking to Ahmed or me. "See ya," she waved as they exited the office.

Pete stepped toward the machine, but I followed Karly into the hallway. I wanted to remind her about practice.

I called to her, "Don't forget . . ." But I stopped when I saw them. Karly and Ahmed were halfway down the hall—and they were holding hands. *Holding hands!*

Back in the office, Pete was already making copies. I leaned up against the wall, my head spinning from what I'd just seen. If Karly and Ahmed were holding hands at school, I'm pretty sure it meant they were a couple. Which made me wonder:

One: Why hadn't Karly told me? My stomach twisted, thinking of her keeping a secret that big.

And two: How could I get there with Kevin?

"I'm going to save some for the shops downtown," Pete said, bringing me back to real time. He lifted the stack of flyers off the machine. "But Ms. Kumar said we should hang some up around school." He handed me half. "We have ten minutes before next period. Where do you want to start?"

"I don't know." I was having trouble focusing on anything other than Karly and Ahmed *holding hands*!

"I'll take the sixth-grade hallway and you could do the seventh," Pete said.

With the stack of flyers in my hand, I headed down the hall, but I couldn't stop thinking about Karly and Ahmed. I was barely paying attention as I tacked a flyer up on the bulletin board across from a long row of lockers. Then I headed toward the music room, but as I passed the art studio, I heard Kevin's voice.

Peering into the room, I saw Ms. McMann, the art teacher, standing at a table with Kevin and Ryan next to her.

"Sash-aaa!" Kevin sang.

"What are you guys doing?" I stepped inside.

"Decorations." Ryan held up his hands. They were coated in goo. "You want to help?"

I eyed a bunch of blown-up balloons on the floor. "That's for the auditorium?"

"Yup." Ryan lifted up a strip of newspaper. I looked over at Kevin.

"The boys have decided on papier–mâché snowmen and hanging snowflakes," Ms. McMann explained as she walked over to the deep sink at the back of the room. "It's an ambitious project."

"Oh, wow. Sorry, though—I can't help right now. I need to finish hanging these flyers." I waved the stack in the air. It seemed silly but I wished Kevin would offer to help me. I hadn't talked to him (not really) since I sent him the text about going to Downtown D'Lights. And after seeing Karly and Ahmed *together* together, I wanted to make sure we were moving ahead too. "I can help tomorrow," I said, standing in the doorway.

I thought Kevin would say something to me then, but he was too busy flicking Ryan with goo.

"That would be great, Sasha." Ms. McMann dried her hands with a paper towel. "Come during lunch." Then she turned toward them. "Boys! Focus!"

I headed down the hall. At least I had a plan for surviving lunch tomorrow. And I would be hanging out with Kevin. Which was really good because Downtown D'Lights Night (a.k.a. our first date!) was only three days away. It was a super important night, especially now that I knew exactly what needed to happen. Kevin and I were going to hold hands.

Chapter Eleven
BAM! BAM! BAM!

As soon as I opened the door to the apartment and saw Mom, I knew she was angry. She stood with the phone to her ear, her lips pressed together. I dropped my bags, hung up my coat, and eyed the door to my room, wondering if I could get there before she started yelling. Mom's lips always tightened before she yelled . . . at Dad. As I slipped inside my room, I heard the words:

"I told you this would happen."

She was definitely talking to Dad.

A few minutes later she knocked on my door. As she stepped inside, I realized Dad wasn't the only one in trouble.

"Have you been on GradeCheck recently?" The online grade book, updated regularly by teachers and checked daily—sometimes hourly—by helicopter parents was, as far as I was concerned, one of the worst inventions ever.

"Yes." I sat on my bed, my back against the headboard. "My science grade dropped two points."

"It's a B." She massaged her temples as if she had a headache, as if my grade was giving her a headache.

"Mom, it's not a big deal It's a B+."

"It's science, Sasha. It is a big deal. Tech Magnet won't consider your application if your science grades aren't excellent."

I wanted to say, *I'm only in seventh grade and I don't even want to go to Tech Magnet*. But instead I said, "I'm like two points away from an A. I can get the grade back up."

"Sasha," Mom sighed. "You're spending too much time on dance."

"What?"

"Yes." She glanced over at my bulletin board. It was filled with recital photos and a High School for the Performing Arts poster. "It's just, it takes up so much of your time. You're practicing every day."

"But Mom, it's the Holidaze Spectacular. It's important." There was no way I was giving up the show. Winning that was my only chance at the Summer Academy. And that was the closest I was ever going to get to the High School for Performing Arts, if Mom had anything to do with it.

"I know, I know. It's important to you. But after the show, I want you to refocus."

"Refocus?"

"Yes, I want you to sign up for the robotics team and the coding course I was telling you about."

"Mom!" She didn't want me to "refocus"—she wanted me to change. I tugged at the pillow behind me, repositioning it. "I'm not Claire."

"I know that, but you need to add some STEM activities and get your science grade up."

I stared straight ahead, not saying anything.

"Sash, I just want you to have choices." Mom headed toward the door as I pulled my earbuds out of my backpack.

Choices? Yeah, me too. Like I wanted to be able to decide how I spend my time and where I apply to high school.

"Are you okay?" Mom asked before leaving.

"Fine." I pushed the earbuds into my ears. But I didn't feel fine. I didn't want to be on a robotics team. I wanted to dance, not code. And I wanted Mom to be proud of *me*, not disappointed that I wasn't like Claire.

On Wednesday during lunch, I headed to the art room to help with decorations.

A bunch of other kids were there too. At the back table, Pete and a couple of his friends from the basketball team were painting the papier–mâché snowmen. (That was nice of him to recruit help. We needed it!) Mira and Anna were working at a table up front. But I didn't see Kevin. Or Ryan.

"Where's Kevin?" I asked Mira, who was very carefully cutting out a cardboard snowflake.

"I think he's in the auditorium. He said something about working on an acro trick with Ryan."

Weird. Kevin must be teaching Ryan how to do something for his act. I tried to shrug it off, but it bugged me that he was spending time helping another performer. Ryan was our competition, and he was going to be tough to beat. I wished Kevin wasn't helping him. *We* were a team—not Ryan and Kevin.

"Here." Mira handed me a white piece of cardboard. "Cut this snowflake, and then put glitter on it."

I got to work but the whole time, I kept glancing over at the door, hoping Kevin would walk in. But he didn't.

"Looks good," Ms. McCann said as I showed her a row of finished snowflakes. "We'll need clear fishing line to hang them from the ceiling."

"I can get that," Pete said from behind me. "We sell it at the store."

"Thanks, Pete," Ms. McMann said. Then she moved toward Mira, who was waving her glitter-covered hand.

"Sasha?" Pete said.

"Oh, hi!" I turned to face him.

"I was wondering . . ." he looked down at his hands, "if you want to work on the promo video sometime? The one you told me about, for the show."

"Sure, yeah." It was really nice that he remembered—I had almost forgotten about it.

"I was thinking we could splice together photos and videos of the different things that go into putting on the show," Pete said. "Like a clip from making the decorations, then of rehearsals, then of hanging up flyers."

"That's a good idea." I brushed a strand of hair off my face. "I'll take some photos."

"Um, you . . ." Pete started to say, and sort of reached toward my face before dropping his hand. "You got glitter on your chin." He grinned.

"Oh, whoops!" I laughed and wiped it off.

"Anyway, maybe we can put it together this weekend. That will give us time to get it out on social media."

"Okay, sure. How about Sunday afternoon?" I couldn't do Saturday. I'd be too busy getting ready for the big date.

"Great!" Pete said. "It's a plan." We smiled at each other, then we went to clean up.

On the way to class, I spotted Kevin in front of me in the hallway but I didn't call to him. The funny thing was, I'd forgotten I'd been looking for him.

After school, I stopped in at the classroom where the Knitting Club met. There were only three members, but they seemed excited about the hat and mitten drive.

"Why don't you put this on the tree?" An eighth-grade boy handed me a blue hat with a big pom-pom. "The tree looks pretty bare. It might help."

"Thanks, this is perfect!" I said. On my way out of school, I put the hat on top of the pink tree. It looked cute, but otherwise the tree really was empty. Well, not totally empty—there was one pair of store-bought mittens. Leaning over, I read the tag. They were from Sugarman's. Pete must've donated them! That made me smile, and I pushed through the school doors feeling good.

Outside, the cold air made my teeth chatter; as I headed to JayJay's, I pulled my fleece neck warmer up over my chin.

On Wednesdays, Karly and I had a dance class focused on leaps, jumps, and turns. But when I arrived in the studio, panting and out of breath from running the last third of the way, Karly wasn't there. As I sashayed across the studio and practiced my stag leaps, I wondered where she was. Our plan was to practice our routine after class. Kevin didn't come to the studio on Wednesdays, so Karly and I were going to walk to the Hall's house and then practice all together for an hour. So where was she?

By the time class ended, I was angry.

Pulling out my phone, I texted her: *Where r u?* I waited, watching for the three dots to appear, but nothing.

Then I texted Kevin: *What's up? R u ready to practice?* Again, I waited and again, nothing.

How could they both blow off practice? Didn't they realize we needed to stick to our schedule? Irritated, I decided I'd head home. There was no point in going to the Hall's house if Karly and Kevin weren't there.

I held my phone in my mitten-covered hand as I walked, so I could see if either of them had texted me, but by the time I reached Sugarman's, neither of them had. Angry and cold, I headed inside to buy a snack. Mom had a late class on Wednesdays, and I wasn't exactly psyched for dinner: microwavable corndogs with a side of freezer burn.

The bells jangled on the door behind me. The warmth of the store made my cheeks tingle as I pulled off my mittens.

"Hey," Pete said from the counter in the back.

Anna was doing her homework at a café table. "Sasha!"

"Hey." I waved to both of them, then looked down at my phone. Still nothing.

I ordered a hot cocoa and a cookie from Mr. Sugarman, and sat down next to Anna.

"Here you go." Pete carried the food and drink over to me.

"Thanks." I took a sip. Yum.

Anna had a page of math problems on the table in front of her, but she was looking at her phone, scrolling through Instagram.

"Don't you need to get your homework done?" I asked.

"Yes, Mom." She rolled her eyes at me. "But check this out." Anna tilted her phone toward me. It was a photo of Ahmed and Karly sipping on straws stuck into the same milk shake. "They're looking pretty cozy, wouldn't you say?"

I reached for the phone. "When was that posted?"

"Two minutes ago."

Seriously? Karly blew off practice to hang out with Ahmed? She didn't even text to tell me. And it didn't look like she was practicing for Quiz Bowl—it looked like she was on a date. I started to fume.

"Wait, where are you going?" Anna said when I

stood to put on my coat. "I thought you could help me with math. And you haven't even finished your cocoa!"

"Call me later," I said, heading to the door.

Back in the apartment, I turned on "Winter Dreams." Without Mom at home, I blasted the music from the speaker in the kitchen, then I pushed back the dining room table and practiced our dance. Maybe Karly and Kevin weren't taking the performance seriously, but I was. By the time I ran through it a third time, my anger started to loosen. And by the fourth time, I was lost in the music. My ponytail whipped from side to side as I headed into the knee drop. And on the floor, I focused on each movement.

I owned it.

Then the pounding began. The music was so loud that at first, I thought it was part of the beat. But then I realized it wasn't coming from the speaker. It was coming from below me.

Bam! Bam! Bam!

My heart sank. It was our downstairs neighbor hitting the end of her broom against the ceiling—her way of telling me to stop.

I turned off the music and flopped onto the sofa, hanging my legs off the arm. Sometimes I hated the apartment. I couldn't even practice without our downstairs neighbors having a tantrum.

When my phone rang, I raced to the counter to pick it up. It was Kevin.

"Hi," I said, trying not to sound annoyed.

"Sasha! I'm sorry I flaked on you today."

"No problem." I was doing my best to keep my voice calm. I was angry, but I didn't want to sound angry.

"We can practice tomorrow. Ms. Kumar said we could use the auditorium after school."

"Oh, that's great!"

"Yeah, I explained to her how because of Quiz Bowl, Karly couldn't practice at lunch."

My anger toward Kevin started to dissolve. "Thanks for doing that."

"Yeah, we need to bring our A game to the competition. I watched a couple of the acts during lunch today, and they're good. I mean, seriously good."

That was what I was afraid of—the competition. "Karly better be there tomorrow."

"She will be. I told her if she didn't show, she'd be making my bed for the next three months."

"Good." Karly hated making her bed. The threat of making Kevin's should motivate her.

"You psyched about Downtown D'Lights?" Kevin asked.

YES. "It's going to be fun!" I said, but didn't add, *especially when you hold my hand.*

"I can't wait to go ice skating and show off my new moves."

Ice skating? Gulp. I had mixed feelings about ice skating on our first date. On the one hand, I couldn't ice skate—I couldn't even stand up for more than three seconds without a face plant on the ice—so it didn't exactly play to my strengths. But on the other hand, I couldn't ice skate—which meant Kevin would need to help me. Which meant it was the surest way for us to hold hands.

"Yeah, me too," I said.

"I heard the Senior Center is bringing back the snowman-making competition. Remember that?"

"Of course." How could I forget? When I was little, it was my favorite event. Claire and I were always partners, and she'd do the wrapping (each pair was given a roll of toilet paper) while I stood very still until my whole body was covered. We'd been the fastest, and won a bunch of times.

Kevin had started talking about what he wanted to

eat (gingerbread cookies, hot chocolate, pizza), but I was only half listening. I was still thinking about the snowman-making at the Senior Center and debating what would be more "date like": wrapping Kevin in toilet paper or being wrapped myself. Okay, maybe neither, but still it would give us a chance to get closer (literally).

"Yoo-hoo, Sash. You still there?"

Startled, I realized I had no idea what Kevin had been saying. "Oops! Yeah!"

By the time the call ended, I wasn't at all angry with him anymore. True, he'd blown off practice, but he'd apologized. Even better, he'd arranged for us to rehearse tomorrow afternoon. Anyway, I couldn't be mad at Kevin. It definitely didn't fit in with my plan for Kevasha.

Karly, though, was a different story.

Chapter Twelve
PREPARATION

"I can't believe you blew off practice yesterday. You didn't even text me." I stood on the stage, looking down at Karly, who sat in the first row, pulling off her boots. "We needed that time to practice." I wasn't yelling, but I also wasn't exactly using what teachers call an "inside voice."

"I know." Karly pulled up her leg warmers. "But I also needed to practice for Quiz Bowl. Sasha, it's one week from this Saturday."

"But you weren't even practicing."

"What are you talking about?" Karly lifted herself onto the stage.

"I saw the picture on Instagram. You weren't studying. You were on a date. With Ahmed."

"A date? I wish. Sasha, we were taking a five-minute break. Do you have any idea how tiring it is to run through a thousand questions and try to solve a bunch of math problems in seconds?" She stared at me. "No, you don't."

"Girls." Ms. Kumar stood in the back of the auditorium. "Is everything okay?"

"Yes," Karly and I said at the exact same time. Normally we would've laughed or said "jinx" when that happened, but instead we glared at each other.

"This is supposed to be fun. Remember?" Ms. Kumar sat down in the second row. "Why don't you show me what you have so far?"

Just then Kevin barged through the auditorium doors, ran down the center aisle, and jumped onto the stage. "I'm here!" He did a pivot turn and faced the audience.

Ms. Kumar laughed. "You sure know how to make an entrance."

"You're not doing that during the show, right?" Karly asked. I was thinking the same thing but instead I said, "Nice."

Karly raised her left eyebrow at me. "Nice? Really?"

I took a deep breath and turned on the music. We ran through the routine but Karly and I bumped into each other doing a turn and Kevin and I were still struggling to reach the high notes of the song. When we finished, Ms. Kumar offered a few suggestions (mostly about my and Kevin's singing) and then we tried it again.

"Better," Ms. Kumar said when we finished.

"It would be even better if you gave me back the hat." Kevin bumped my arm with his. "You've got to admit, it would give my costume just the spark it needs."

"Spark?" Karly and I said at the same time in the same skeptical tone. This time, we both cracked a smile.

"You two have no vision. You need to shake it up," he said as he did a shimmy with his shoulders.

"I've got to go." Karly climbed off the stage. "Quiz Bowl meeting."

"Now?" I said. "But I thought we could work on our costumes." We still needed to glue the candy cane appliqués onto the white leotards.

"Sorry." She zipped up her coat and swung her backpack over her shoulder. "I can't be late."

"How about—" I was about to ask Kevin if he wanted to work on it when Ryan burst through the door.

"Hi, Ryan." Ms. Kumar waved from her seat in the second row. "You ready to do your run-through?"

"Sorry, Sash." Kevin yanked Ryan up on the stage. "I promised I'd help with some of his acro moves."

"Wait, what?" I asked as Kevin and Ryan pulled out a mat from backstage. "Why?"

It was Ms. Kumar who spoke. "Kevin is going to make a cameo appearance in Ryan's act. So they can do a few stunts."

"But . . ." Annoyed, I scooted off the edge of the stage.

"Sasha," Ms. Kumar said as I approached the second row. "It's not a problem. Kevin can be in both acts."

Not a problem? Not a problem for whom? I grabbed my boots, backpack, and coat and headed out of the auditorium.

"See ya, Sasha!" Kevin called from the stage.

On a bench in the hallway, I sat down to put on my boots. As I struggled to get my right heel in, I suddenly felt like crying. I knew Mom would say "It's your hormones," but it wasn't that. I was angry—it was obvious Kevin and Karly weren't taking our performance seriously enough—but there was something else jumbled in there with my anger, too. I was hurt. With Kevin spending more time on acro and Karly doing Quiz Bowl, they'd found new friends. Karly had even found a boyfriend. Was I being replaced?

Not wanting to cry, I rubbed my eyes and stood up.

I didn't know what I was going to do about Karly. But with Kevin, I was determined to move us to the next level. Wouldn't being boyfriend-girlfriend be even better than best friends?

I needed our date to go perfectly. As with any big test, preparation was key. I needed to outline what we would do leading up to the big moment when we'd hold hands.

Geeky? Yes, but that's why I made it on to the high honor roll every semester. Preparation.

I zipped up my coat and headed outside.

At the Senior Center on Saturday, Karly wasn't there again. As I helped serve lunch, I was determined to not let Karly's absence (and lack of text about it) get to me. Tonight was Downtown D'Lights and I needed to stay focused. I'd already laid out my clothes for it—jeans and my superfuzzy blue sweater. And I'd printed out a list of conversation starters (thank you, Google) in case there were any awkward moments. Most importantly, on a small index card, I'd written the order of events for the night and the likelihood of reaching my goal.

1. Snowman-Making Competition at the Senior Center (chance of holding hands: unlikely)
2. Dinner at Salvatore's (chance of holding hands: possible)
3. Ice Skating (chance of holding hands: definite)

I wasn't the only one at the Senior Center thinking about Downtown D'Lights. The staff was busy setting up for the events they were hosting. In the dining room, there would be make-your-own gingerbread houses using graham crackers, frosting, and gumdrops. In the lounge, there would be a storytime for preschoolers, and in the yoga room there would be a snowman-making contest. I smiled when I spotted a huge box of toilet paper in there.

After lunch, I hung up some posters for the Holidaze Spectacular. Big T and Miss Melinda sat in a circle with five other people in the lounge area. They were all knitting, which reminded me of the mitten and hat drive at school. The tree was still pretty bare. I went over and told the group about the drive, and they were super enthusiastic.

"No problem," Big T said. "We'll get to work on it right away."

"Sasha." Miss Melinda handed me a hat. "This is for you."

For me? It was really cute—a black cap with a small red flower embroidered on the front.

"I was going to give it to you for the holidays but now seemed like a good time."

"Wow, thank you!" It was so soft. "I love it." I felt special knowing she'd made it just for me.

"I'm so happy you like it." She smiled.

I gave Miss Melinda a hug. "Thank you so much." I definitely needed a hat, and now I had the perfect one. "I'll wear it tonight."

"Do you have a big date?" Miss Melinda nudged my arm. "For D'Lights Night?"

Embarrassed, I mumbled, "Sort of."

"I'm glad one of us does," Miss Melinda said, winking at Big T. Everyone laughed, including me.

A big date! I couldn't stop thinking about it. Tonight Kevin and I would officially exit the friend zone. Tonight was the start of Kevasha!

At four o'clock, I stood in front of the bathroom mirror and did my makeup. With the exception of dance recitals, where the rule was "the more the better," I didn't usually wear makeup. I started with foundation and then dotted cover-up on a couple of zits. By the time I brushed the blush across my cheeks, I was feeling pretty good but when I was done, I checked my face in the mirror and I wasn't so sure. The foundation looked too light and the eyeliner made my eyes look a little mean. Not exactly the look I was going for. I decided to FaceTime Claire.

"Where are you?" she asked.

"The bathroom. I need you to check my makeup." I turned my face from side to side. "How does it look?"

"Too much blush," Claire said. "And that eyeliner, it's got to go—and the foundation—"

"What should I do?" I rubbed my cheeks and looked at my hands. They were streaked with tan-colored foundation. I was starting to freak out.

"Wash your face."

"What?"

"Yeah. Wash it all off. All you need is a little lip gloss or maybe just some lip balm."

"That's it?"

"It's cold there, right?"

"Freezing."

"Your cheeks will be rosy from being outside." On the screen, she touched her chin. "Just put a little cover up on that."

With my hand, I covered the zit on my chin. "Okay."

After the call ended, I did what Claire told me to do. And without the thick layer of makeup, I felt much better. Much more me.

When I stepped out of the bathroom, Mom looked up from her laptop and smiled. "You're growing up, Sash. I remember the first time we took you to Downtown D'Lights—you were in a stroller. And now look at you, heading off with your friends."

"With Kevin," I corrected her. "Just the two of us. We're going together."

"Right," Mom said. But I was surprised. I thought she'd get all gushy about this being my first date, but she didn't. "Have fun, and don't forget to thank Mrs. Hall for driving you."

At the door, I zipped up my coat. "Mom, are you going to go to any of the events?" I suddenly felt sad about Mom being alone in the apartment on a night that had always been something fun we did as a family.

"Not this year." She tapped the textbook next to her. "With exams coming up, I need to study."

"Okay." I put my hand on the doorknob.

"Please tell me you're wearing a hat," Mom said.

I pivot-turned as I put on the black hat Miss Melinda made for me. "Ta-da!"

"Cute!" Mom gave me a thumb-up. "Very cute." And although I didn't exactly think of Mom as a fashionista, her approval still made me feel good.

"They're here." I looked down at a text from Kevin. "Bye!"

Halfway down the stairs, my stomach started to flutter. I'd never been on a date before! I was excited, but nervous too. Sure, it was only Kevin. But Kevin wasn't just Kevin anymore.

Failure was not an option.

Chapter Thirteen

DOWNTOWN DELIGHTS AND DISASTERS

I'd ridden in the Hall's station wagon a hundred times before, but seeing it parked in front of the building that night, I felt as excited as if it were a stretch limo waiting for me. As I neared the car door, I inhaled deeply, doing a yoga breath. It usually helped calm my nerves, but the coldness of the air surprised me and when I exhaled, I started coughing uncontrollably.

"You okay?" Kevin asked, peering around from the front seat as I slid into the backseat.

"Yeah." I was relieved the coughing had stopped, but I was disappointed Kevin was in the front seat. I'd imagined the two of us in the backseat together.

Mrs. Hall turned around too. "Sasha, I love your hat!"

"Thank you." I touched the embroidered flower. "Miss Melinda, at the Senior Center, gave it to me. She made it."

"Wow!" Kevin said. "That's really nice. If only I had the top hat, then we'd really be stylin'."

"Top hat?" Mrs. Hall asked as she started driving.

"Ryan gave me this awesome top hat. He thought it would be good for the Holidaze Spectacular."

"That was nice of him," Mrs. Hall said.

"Yeah, wasn't it? But Sasha vetoed it. She said it was too much."

"Hmm." Mrs. Hall glanced at me in the rearview mirror. "I think I'll side with Sasha on this one."

"Mrs. Hall, if you saw it . . ." I shook my head and shivered.

"You'd love it, Mom." Kevin faced me. "You *are* going to give it back to me, right?"

"Right after the show, it's all yours."

Kevin groaned; Mrs. Hall and I laughed.

"Do you want me to drive you to the top of Main Street or do you want to start somewhere else?" Mrs. Hall asked.

"The ice skating rink." Kevin turned in his seat to face me. "Right?"

"Actually . . ." I needed to stick to my schedule. "I was thinking we could start with the snowman-making contest at the Senior Center. Is that okay?"

"Sure."

"Oh, I remember that one," Mrs. Hall said, laughing. "That's when you wrap your partner in toilet paper and then decorate them like a snowman."

As we drove through town, Mrs. Hall turned up the radio. She and Kevin sang along to a corny holiday song, hamming up the chorus. I looked out the window at the houses decked out with holiday decorations. Lights, inflatable dreidels and Santas, and life-size reindeer. My favorite lights were the white ones—not the *white*-white ones, but the ones with the warm golden glow. That's the kind we decorated our old house with. Claire and I would trail behind Dad as he strung the lights over the bushes, and then we'd stand on the ground handing him strands of lights as he climbed a ladder to reach the top of the big pine tree.

When Mrs. Hall turned down Main Street, I spotted Anna and Mira on the crowded sidewalk. Main Street hadn't seen this many people since, well, last year's Downtown D'Lights.

Mrs. Hall dropped us off in front of the Senior Center. "Call me if you need a ride. Dad and I will be shopping, but who knows, maybe we'll join you later at the ice skating rink."

"Ahh. Please don't," Kevin said. Then he leaned over and kissed her on the cheek.

"Have fun, and if you see Karly, she'd better be wearing a hat."

"Karly's here?" I asked Kevin as we headed up the steps.

"Did you think she'd miss D'Lights Night?"

"No." I knew Karly loved it. Last year, she'd made the entire Hall family walk around wearing elf hats. "But . . ."

"She's with the team." He shrugged. "Even Quiz Bowlers need a study break, I guess."

Thinking about Karly hanging out with her new friends (and boyfriend!) bothered me. I knew it shouldn't, especially since it made it much easier for me to be on a date with Kevin. But still . . . Karly hadn't even asked what I was doing for Downtown D'Lights. She also hadn't said anything about she and Ahmed being a couple.

"Come on." Kevin pulled me into the lobby where there were carolers and a display of gingerbread houses. "Let's do this."

A few minutes later, Miss Melinda handed me a roll of toilet paper, a scrap of fleece, and a hat. "Good luck, Sasha." The room was crowded with teams. I sized up our competition: there were a couple of Senior Center regulars, a few teenagers, and everyone else was under the age of ten.

"We can win this," I whispered to Kevin.

"I don't know." He nodded toward a small child crawling on the ground. "The competition looks pretty fierce."

"Ha." I shook the roll of toilet paper in my hand. "You better stand still."

"Kevin!" A little kid Kevin and Karly had babysat for bounded into the room. "Can you be my partner? Please, please." He tugged on Kevin's sleeve.

"Of course, buddy. You can join our team."

What? This was not what I planned.

"Mine!" The little kid grabbed the roll of toilet paper from my hand.

"Go!" Miss Melinda called as a song about a snowman blasted into the room.

You've got to be kidding me! I thought as the little kid (apparently our partner) threw the roll of toilet paper over Kevin's head. What a fail! I wasn't going to get close to Kevin, and to top it off, we were going to lose.

"Here." I picked up the roll. "Why don't I do his head and shoulders." I stepped forward to start wrapping but the kid yelled, "No! I want to do it!"

Sighing, I handed him the roll of toilet paper.

"You can do it, buddy," Kevin said but the kid bent over and started wrapping his own knees.

"I want to be the snowman," he said.

"No problem." Kevin reached for the roll. "We can wrap you up real fast."

Let's start with his mouth, I thought.

"No!" The kid pulled the toilet paper back. "I want to do it myself."

Kevin, whose knees were still wrapped in toilet paper, shrugged his shoulders. "Sure."

Kevin and I watched as the kid wrapped a wad of toilet paper around his own neck and then started on his ankles. A few seconds later, the winners were announced—a husband and wife who were Senior Center regulars.

"You made me lose!" the little kid said to us as he ran out of the room. The toilet paper still stuck to him. Kevin and I looked at each other and cracked up.

"Remind me to let Karly babysit for him alone next time."

"Dance Party!" Big T called as he cranked the music. Then everyone in the room danced. The snowmen busted out of their wrappings. Shredded toilet paper flew into the air. We laughed as sheets of tissue paper fell onto our heads. Kevin wadded up a bunch and threw it at me as if it were a snowball. I ducked, and then scooped some off the floor.

Kevin did a jig. "You can't catch me."

"Got you!" I said, hitting him with a wad of toilet paper.

"How about decorating cupcakes at the bakery?" Kevin pointed down the block as we walked along Main Street, checking out the window displays and the lights. "I think I saw Ryan—"

"Um." Ryan? No way. I was determined to stick to my schedule and I was not interested in running into any of our friends. "I thought we could get dinner at Salvatore's?"

"Sure," Kevin said. "You know me." He patted his puffy coat. "I'm always hungry."

But as soon as we stepped inside Salvatore's, Anna and Mira called to us from a booth. Shoot!

"Help us finish this," Mira said as we approached. "We should've ordered slices, but Anna insisted we order a whole pizza." Mira clutched her stomach.

"You're the one who wanted the meat lover's," Anna said. "So don't blame me if you have indigestion."

"Looks great to me." Kevin plopped down in the booth next to Mira.

Anna scooted over; reluctantly, I sat next to her. This was definitely not the cozy dinner for two I'd imagined. The chance of Kevin and I holding hands during dinner just went from possible to impossible.

Kevin grabbed a slice, folded the sides inward, and took a bite.

"Here." Anna handed me a plate while Kevin picked up Mira's soda and took a big gulp.

"Sure, no problem, Kev." Mira rolled her eyes. "Next time, could you ask?"

Orange-colored pizza grease seeped onto my paper plate, and I picked off the sausage pieces from my slice.

"I'll eat those." Kevin put down Mira's soda and popped a piece of sausage into his mouth, then licked his fingers.

I'd forgotten what a gross eater Kevin could be— snarfing his food like a vacuum cleaner. He was also infamous for his long-lasting burps (his record was seventeen seconds, and yes, he'd timed it).

As if on cue, Kevin burped.

"Gross," Anna said. I made a face.

"Oops." He looked over at me. "Sorry."

Nothing was going the way I planned. But still we had ice skating, which I'd figured was my best chance for hand-holding anyway. But Kevin definitely needed to wash his hands first.

I ate a slice, and despite the pepperoni overkill, it tasted good.

"After this, you guys want to go to the Karaoke station?" Mira asked.

"Yup." Kevin grabbed another piece. "For sure."

"Uh . . ." I looked over at Kevin. "I thought we'd go ice skating next."

"You? Ice skating?" Anna turned toward me. "Sash, you said you were never going again. Remember?"

I remembered. The last time I'd skated (if that's what you could call my sad combination of shuffling and falling, shuffling and falling) was at Mira's eleventh birthday party. But this was different. I had a goal and this was the best way to reach it.

"Yeah, well." I looked over at Kevin, chewing on the crust. "He's going to teach me."

"I am?" Kevin asked, his mouth full of food.

"You are." I nodded.

"Good luck with that!" Mira winked at Kevin as she and Anna stood.

"I know why Sasha wants to go skating." Anna zipped up her coat.

Oh no . . . was Anna about to say I wanted to go so I could hold hands with Kevin? She would definitely start teasing us . . . but I secretly hoped she'd come up with "Kevasha" on her own.

"Why?" Mira asked.

"She wants to check out the hot chocolate stand." Anna bumped Mira's arm. "You know, Pete Sugarman."

"What?" Kevin sprayed soda from his mouth onto the table. "Sasha has a crush on Pete?"

"No! No I don't. I—" But there was nothing I could say. They weren't listening. The three of them kept cracking up as they tried different ways of combining my name with Pete.

"Pete-asha," Kevin said. "That's it."

My heart dropped. How had things gone this wrong? Now Kevin thought I liked Pete!

"Totally," Mira said.

"Petasha, Petasha," the three of them chanted.

"Stop! No!" I covered my ears, but it was useless.

"Petasha!" Kevin's voice was loudest of all.

Chapter Fourteen
FALLING

Out on the ice, Kevin skated fast. He circled the rink with smooth crossover turns while I shuffled along with one hand gripping the wall. In front of me, a toddler inched along. She was about a thousand times steadier than me. Talk about embarrassing. This was a terrible idea.

"Wait up!" I called as Kevin whizzed past again.

"How can you be such a good dancer but such a bad skater?" Kevin did an impressive hockey stop in front of me.

"Ice." I pushed off with my blade and teetered forward. "I don't dance on ice."

"Watch." Kevin glided forward. I followed behind him, wobbling, my arms stretching out toward him.

Kevin waited for me, and when I reached him, he linked his arm with mine.

Yes! This was the best idea! Side by side, we glided forward. I was feeling good—until I spotted three preschoolers who were holding on to crates directly in front of us. I was headed right toward them, and fast. Taking out three little kids in an epic crash was not my goal for the night!

"Kevin?" I wasn't sure what was shaking more—my voice or my legs. "We're going to . . ."

"Going to what?" Kevin said. One of the preschoolers was only a foot away. I closed my eyes but Kevin grabbed hold of my arm and steered us around them. When I opened my eyes, they were behind us—all three kids, all three crates—still upright. Phew.

We skated around and around the rink. Well, Kevin skated and I clung to his arm, hoping I wouldn't fall.

"You know I don't have a crush on Pete." I nodded toward the banner above Sugarman's Hot Chocolate Stand set up between the lit Christmas tree and the giant, unlit menorah (Hanukkah didn't start for a few more days).

"Sash, you told me. Like, twenty times on the way over here. It's not a big deal."

"But I don't. I like . . ." I was about to say *you—I like you*, but just then a little kid buzzed by me, which made me lose my balance. I lurched forward.

"Whoa." Kevin grabbed my waist, saving me from the ice. As I straightened back up, his hand reached out for mine—and then it was happening—the very thing I'd been hoping for all night. We were holding hands.

Well, our wool mittens were holding hands, but still . . .

"Hey!" Ryan called, skating toward us.

Ryan? Seriously? Right now? Talk about bad timing! How was I going to keep Kevin focused on me? They would probably want to try their new acro stunts on the ice, or something, and then I would be left watching.

"Hey!" Kevin lifted our hands into the air to wave at him.

At least we were still holding hands.

Until Ryan tagged the back of Kevin's coat, said, "You're it," and sped away.

Kevin dropped my hand and chased after Ryan. I shuffled toward the wall, but about six feet away from it, a girl careened into me, knocking me down onto the ice.

"Sorry!" she called over her shoulder.

Ouch. I straightened my hat and then tried to get back up. But after two attempts, I still wasn't on my feet, and the cold was starting to seep through my mittens and jeans.

On my knees, I crawled toward the wall. Skaters whizzed by all around me.

"You okay?" a boy half my age asked.

"No."

It was official—I'd crossed over from embarrassment to total humiliation. Plus, I was pretty sure I had frostbite on the tip of my nose.

"You want help?" The boy's little arms stretched toward me.

"No," I said, but I did. I wanted Kevin's help. But Kevin hadn't even noticed I'd fallen.

The kid shrugged his shoulders and skated away.

Clutching the wall, I stood up. My feet ached, especially my toes. I tried to wiggle them, but they were numb from the cold, or maybe the skates were too tight. Either way, I couldn't feel them.

Against the flow of all the other skaters, I inched toward the exit, gripping the top of the wall.

"Where are you going?" Kevin asked, skating toward me.

"To sit down." I pointed to the benches. But by the time I finished the sentence, he was already gone, racing after Ryan.

At the exit, I turned back toward the rink. Kevin was only a foot away from Ryan. He reached out his hand to tag him, but Ryan pushed ahead just in time. They were both so good at skating, their game of tag could take all night.

On the bench, I unlaced my skates and wiggled some feeling back into my toes. The rink was crowded and a few other kids joined Kevin and Ryan's game of tag. I laughed as a little boy finally tagged Ryan, then sped away. Kevin held a little girl's hand as they skated ahead of Ryan, trying not to get caught. When Ryan neared, Kevin blocked the girl so she wouldn't be tagged. When Ryan hit the back of Kevin's puffy coat, they all skated away from Kevin and another round began.

I heard Karly's laugh before I saw her. I turned around, and there she was—wearing ice skates, walking toward the rink. Other members of the Quiz Bowl teetered next to her.

"Hey," I said as she passed by.

"Oh, hey!" Startled, she stopped at the bench. "I didn't see you there. Where's Kevin? He told me the two of you were hanging out."

I pointed to the rink, where Kevin landed a toe loop jump.

"He's such a show-off." Karly scratched her nose with her gloved finger. "And he's met his perfect match." She pointed to Ryan. "He's a show-off too."

"You coming?" Ahmed asked her as he passed.

"Yeah." She looked down at my skates. "You want to skate with us?"

"Nah, I'll wait for Kevin."

"You sure? It could be a while."

"I'm good," I said. But as minutes passed, I felt colder and colder. Watching Kevin and Ryan trying to one-up each other was starting to get annoying. And then there was the Quiz Bowl team: Most of them weren't that much better than me, but unlike me, they looked like they were having fun. With Karly in the middle, they formed a line, linking arms. When Ahmed wobbled, bringing all of them crashing onto the ice, they all were laughing hysterically. Then, when one would stand up, another one would fall back down, but they never stopped laughing and smiling.

A kid sat down on the bench next to me to drink his hot chocolate. It smelled good. It looked good too—a perfect swirl of whipped cream rose from the cup.

I glanced over at the stand. There was a long line, maybe ten people deep. I saw the kid next to me take another sip, which left a mustache of chocolate above his lip. A cup of warm hot chocolate sounded really good. I decided to go get some.

I returned my rental skates, put on my boots, and headed over to the stand.

"Sasha!" Mr. Sugarman called, gesturing for me to approach the table.

"Hi, Mr. Sugarman." I stood next to the line, wondering why he'd called me over.

"Would you be willing to help Pete while I run back to the store and get more whipped cream?"

"Sure!" I was happy to help Mr. Sugarman. Plus, it sure beat freezing my butt off on the bench. I looked over at Pete, who was filling up a cup.

"Hey, Sasha," Pete said, and smiled at me. "It's

pretty easy back here—we just fill them up." He pointed to the thermos, "and hand them out."

"Got it!" I said, grabbing an empty cup from the tall stack.

At first the line grew longer, and at one point it seemed like Pete's entire basketball team showed up, but we worked quickly, and soon there were only a couple of people in line. Then there was no one.

"Break time." As Pete poured us each a cup of hot chocolate, I realized that for the past fifteen minutes, I hadn't even thought about being cold or about Kevin. The work had warmed me up. I'd even taken my coat off.

"Sorry, no peppermint," Pete said, grinning, as he handed me the cup.

"I'm sure it will still be delicious. Thanks." We clinked cups and then each took a sip. Mmm . . . just as good as I'd hoped. My face felt warm as I smiled back at Pete.

The sound of someone clearing his throat made us turn toward the counter at the same time. It was Ryan, and standing next to him was Kevin.

"Sorry to interrupt," Ryan said, winking at me and bumping Kevin's shoulder with his. "It looks like things are heating up at the hot chocolate stand." Ugh, Kevin had told him the whole Petasha joke. I rolled my eyes.

"Huh?" Pete looked at Ryan, and then Kevin. "Do you guys want hot chocolate?"

"Yeah," Ryan said. "Two, please."

When I handed Kevin a cup, he mouthed something to me. Did he just say "*I like you*"?

What? I mouthed back.

He did it again, but I couldn't tell for sure.

What? I mouthed again.

He leaned forward, cupping his hand around my ear, and I swallowed nervously as I waited to hear what he said.

"*Petasha!*" he whispered in my ear.

Nooooo! I wanted to scream.

But I said nothing as I watched Kevin—who was supposed to be my date!—laughing with his new best friend, and then walking away from me. What a fail.

Chapter Fifteen
PETASHA AND OTHER PROBLEMS

Beep . . . *beep* . . . the sound of an incoming text woke me the next morning. *Beep* . . . *beep*. I grabbed my phone from the bedside table (I'd forgotten to park it on the kitchen counter before I went to sleep, and Mom was so focused on studying, she hadn't noticed). The text was from Anna.

Anna? She was seriously the last person I wanted to hear from. Thanks to her ridiculous idea that Pete and I should be a thing, my first date had turned into a total disaster.

Anna: *OMG Petasha 2 cute*

STOP, I texted back, then stashed the phone under my pillow. I didn't want to talk to anyone and

I certainly didn't want to look at any more photos of Kevin having fun at Dowtown D'Lights without me. Last night, my Instagram feed was full of them: Kevin and Ryan singing Karaoke, Kevin and Ryan decorating cupcakes, Kevin and Ryan doing handstands under the lit Christmas tree. Enough already.

True. I'd left early, right after Mr. Sugarman returned to the hot chocolate stand with the whipped cream. But when I started walking home, Kevin called, "Bye, Sasha! See ya tomorrow!" He said it like it was no big deal—like my leaving was no big deal. Which I was pretty sure was not how you should be acting toward your date.

How was I going to get Kevin and me back on track? He needed to know I liked *him*, not Pete.

Claire would know. She was the one person I wanted to talk to, but as I was about to call her, I stopped, realizing she would still be fast asleep in California. Waking up my sister was never a good idea. I'd have to wait.

Closing my eyes, I pulled the blanket over my head. Basically, I wanted to stay there all day, but I couldn't. Pete and I were meeting to work on the promo video for the show, then I was heading over to Karly and Kevin's to practice our routine.

Groaning, I pushed off the blanket and sat up. I did a deep yoga breath—inhale for four, exhale for five—then stretched my arms over my head, bent forward, and then slowly came back up. I felt better, or at least good enough to search through my pile of already worn clothes to find the "cleanest" of my dirty yoga pants.

"Looks like someone needs to do laundry," Mom said from the dining room table, giving me a once-over. "Do you have your darks sorted? I'll start with those."

Sorted? "Not yet." I grabbed my dance bag and headed to the hall closet for my coat. "I'll do it later."

"Sash, later doesn't work for me. If you don't bring them now, you're doing your own laundry this week."

I dropped my dance bag. I hated the building's laundry room; the less time I spent in the basement, the better.

"Fine." I stomped back to get my laundry, shutting my door a little too hard.

"Sasha!" Mom yelled.

"Sorry," I mumbled as I moved around my room, stuffing dirty clothes into the laundry bag. I might've been on top of a lot of things in my life, but keeping my laundry situation under control wasn't one of them.

"Here." I dragged the overflowing bag into the living room.

Mom stood with her basket, eyeing my load. "Uh . . . you can carry that down yourself."

"But I'm late!"

"Then hurry up."

I followed her down the stairs to the basement, where the smell of perfumed detergent was not enough to cover up the stench of mildew.

"Here," I said as I propped my bag against the one open washer.

"You know what I want for Christmas?" Mom said.

"What?"

"Our own washing machine."

I wanted to say, *We used to have one, back at our house*—the house where I could dance in my room without a downstairs neighbor yelling at me, the house where we had a laundry room, and the only reason to go to the basement was to get Halloween decorations. But I stopped myself.

"Thanks, Mom, for doing my laundry."

"Okay. Now, go get your project done." She shooed me toward the stairs.

On my way over to Sugarman's Market I texted Pete

to see if he wanted to meet in the library instead. It would be quieter, I wrote, and Pete agreed. But the real reason I wanted to go to the library was so no one would see us if we worked in one of the study rooms on the second floor. The last thing I needed was for my friends to spot us together and make a big deal out of it.

If Kevin and I had a chance, I needed to put an end to the Petasha rumors.

"What's up, Sasha?" Ryan stood near the circulation desk at the library.

My heart sank. Sometimes it felt like Ryan was everywhere I didn't want him to be.

"Hi," I said in my chilliest voice.

"You looking for Pete?"

I stared at him, bracing myself to be teased, but his tone of voice sounded normal, and he wasn't wink-winking at me.

"Yeah." I started to relax. Maybe he'd forgotten about Petasha. Maybe everyone had. I hoped.

"He's on the second floor, near the study rooms." Ryan raised his left eyebrow, and winked with his right eye.

Shoot! I knew it. The Petasha thing wasn't going to be that easy to beat.

"So now you're studying together?" he said as if it was a date. "Nice."

"Shut up," I said. "You don't know what you're talking about."

"I don't? It looks pretty obvious to me." He smirked, and made a smooching sound.

"Jerk," I said as I headed up the stairs. On the second level, I searched the bookracks and the desks for anyone else I knew. All clear.

When I found Pete, I nodded to an open study room. "Let's work in there."

"Sure." Pete stepped into the room. I glanced around the second floor, making sure no one had seen us.

"You okay?" Pete asked.

"I'm fine." I closed the door and sat down at the table.

"It's just, you left kind of quickly last night." Pete sat down across from me and unzipped his backpack. "I wasn't sure if you didn't feel good or something, or if you were mad because my grandfather roped you into working."

"What? No! I liked working with you—I mean, I liked being at the hot chocolate stand." My words and thoughts were tripping me up. "I was glad I could help. It was just . . . other stuff."

"Okay . . .?" Pete smiled, and I noticed what a nice smile it was. Not smirky or fake.

"Really—I had fun! It was actually the best part of my whole night." As I said that, I realized that it was true. "Is it warm in here? My face feels hot."

"A little, I guess. Do you want me to open the door?" Pete stood.

"No, no. I'm okay." I didn't want one of my friends to spot us and embarrass me.

"You sure?"

"Yup."

"Let me show you what I have so far." Pete sat down next to me, pulling his computer between us.

"Is that new?" I pointed to the computer. It really was warm in there; even my toes felt like they were sweating.

"Yeah," Pete said shyly, as if he didn't want to sound like he was bragging. "My grandfather gave it to me early."

"It's really nice." I couldn't stand the heat a second more; I stood up. "Sorry, it's too hot." I opened the door a crack, and then sat back down.

Pete started showing me the photos and video clips he'd taken. They were all really good. He had a way of making everything—even me cutting out a snowflake—look artistic. I pulled out my phone and showed him what I had.

"That's a great shot," he said, pointing to a photo of Kevin leaping across the stage. Then we talked about which images would be the best to use and in what order. Once we made those decisions, Pete started to put it together.

"What are you thinking about for the music?" he asked.

"How about that new Simin Kurji song? Have you heard it? It's got a great beat."

"I love that song." Pete pulled it up on his phone and soon the two of us were bobbing our heads and humming. "It's perfect."

A knock on the door startled us. Pete turned off the music as I whirled around guiltily, expecting to see a librarian asking us to keep it down. But it wasn't a librarian. It was Anna, peeking her head into the room.

"Hi guys!" She stepped inside. "What are you two

working on?" Her wide smile made me worried about what was going to come out of her mouth next.

"A promo video for the show," Pete said.

"Nothing," I said at the exact same time.

"You two are so cute." She lifted up her phone. "Let me take your photo."

"Please don't—" But I wasn't fast enough. Anna had already taken the picture.

"This is a great one, don't you think?" She tilted her phone toward Pete, who was blushing.

"Sure," he said, sounding like he didn't know what to say.

I stood up. "I'm late for rehearsal," I said. I wasn't, but I needed to leave before things got any more embarrassing. "I gotta go."

"After my game, I'll email you the link." Pete stood up too. "So you can take a look at what we have so far."

"Thanks." I headed toward the door, my coat hanging half off me, my bag unzipped.

"Cute one," Anna was still looking down at her phone as I passed by her. "I'm definitely adding that to my story."

"Story?" Pete said. "What story?"

I turned around to face Anna. "Do *not* add that to your Snapchat story." I glared at Anna. "Understand?"

"I understand perfectly." She winked at me and mouthed *Petasha*.

Ugh! I stomped out of the room and down the main stairs of the library. Once Kevin saw that photo, how was I ever going to get Kevasha back on track?

"Sasha, I'm sorry we missed you at the ice skating rink last night," Mr. Hall said as I hung my coat in the closet. "You should've seen us. Mrs. Hall and I put on quite a show." He lifted his foot an inch off the ground and twirled.

"Honey," Mrs. Hall said, putting her arm around his shoulder. "I don't think Sasha's idea of entertainment includes you disco dancing on the ice."

I laughed and headed to the basement.

Karly was waiting for me at the bottom step. One look at her face told me something was wrong.

"You okay?" I glanced around the studio, trying to find Kevin, but he wasn't there. "Where's Kev?"

"He's coming." Karly sat down on the bottom step. "I wanted to talk to you first."

"Yeah?" I sat next to her. "What's up?" My mind

raced through the possible reasons why Karly looked so serious. Had Kevin confided in her? Maybe he'd told her he liked me and he was hurt because he thought I liked Pete? Or . . .

"Sash, I don't want you to be mad."

Mad? It was then I noticed that she was wearing jeans and not her dance shorts and cropped t-shirt.

"I can't practice today."

"But—"

"I can't practice at all this week."

I stood up. "Are you serious? We have less than two weeks to get ready."

"I know, but things are getting really intense with Quiz Bowl. It's in six days—"

"Karly, you made a commitment to us, to our routine. Remember we want to win the Holidaze Spectacular? This is our dream."

Karly didn't look at me. In her hands, she held a stack of Post-it notes (more Quiz Bowl questions). "The thing is, Sasha, I'm not sure I want to spend so much time on dance."

"What are you talking about? Is this because your pointe shoes are too tight?"

"No. It's just that I want to try other activities."

She looked up at me. "And I've been thinking I might want to apply to Tech Magnet for high school."

"Tech Magnet?" What was Karly talking about? Tech Magnet was not a part of our dream.

"Yeah, Ahmed says they have a really cool maker space and a top robotics team."

"Ahmed says?" Who cares what Ahmed says? "Do you even like robotics?"

"I think it sounds fun."

"Fun?" Was she kidding?

"Yeah, it does. I'm going to join the school team. Ahmed said it'll look good on my Tech Magnet application."

"You know Tech Magnet doesn't even have a dance program?"

"I know, Sash. That's what I'm trying to tell you. I don't care. I don't want to spend so much time on dance. I want to do other things."

"You're quitting? This is your way of telling me you don't want to be in the show anymore?"

"Sasha, I know how much you care about winning the scholarship, and I don't want to mess it up for you, but maybe I could—"

"You're out." I pushed past her and ran up the stairs. I could barely see straight. "Tell Kevin I'll rework the routine without you."

"Sasha!" she called, but I didn't turn back. As I opened the front door, I heard Kevin say, "Where's she going?"

Stomping down the street, I wished I could rewind the last two weeks. I wished Karly had never been selected for the Quiz Bowl A Team. I wished Anna had never shipped Pete Sugarman and me. Then I would be in the Hall's basement studio with Kevin and Karly practicing our routine, perfecting our grand jettes. I wished . . .

The wind whipped at my face. My eyes watered. My ears stung.

I wished I'd worn my hat.

Chapter Sixteen
A PERFECT PLAN

"Sasha, Karly didn't do this to hurt you," Mom said, using her soft voice. "She's doing this because it's the right thing for her." Mom folded a washcloth and added it to the stack of towels on the dining room table. "She wants to spend more time on other interests." Mom grabbed more clothes from the basket of clean laundry.

"Quitting after you've made a commitment to something is not okay," I said.

"It happens." Mom laid a t-shirt on the table. "Sometimes people make decisions that are the right thing for them, but feel like the wrong thing for you."

She brushed off a piece of lint. "People change. That's life."

I was pretty sure Mom wasn't just talking about Karly then.

She went on. "And when that happens, you need to adjust and come up with a new plan. Like how after the divorce, I went back to school. And that's why I'm working so hard, studying all the time—so I can get a good job." She pointed to the piles of clean laundry on the table. "You know, so we can buy a washing machine." She was trying to make a joke but I wasn't ready to laugh. I was angry—angry at Karly, angry at my mom and dad, even angry at Claire (she chose to go to college in California over staying close to me)—angry at all of them for making decisions that were all about what they wanted and nothing about me.

"You need a plan B," Mom said as I reached into the basket of clean clothes and pulled out my favorite jeans.

"Yeah." I'd spent the afternoon working on Plan B: choreographing the routine without Karly's part, rearranging the singing solos. But that wasn't what I wanted. I wanted the original plan, the one where

Karly, Kevin, and I wowed the judge, won the Summer Academy scholarships and eventually danced our way into the High School for Performing Arts.

"You okay?" Mom asked.

"No." I touched the soft fabric of my worn jeans. "I wish everyone would just stop changing."

Mom smiled then, one of her annoying, all-knowing smiles. "But Sasha, you're changing too."

I folded the rest of my laundry in silence.

After dinner, Claire called. At first, I wondered if Mom had already talked to her about what happened with Karly, but when I told her, she sounded surprised.

"Don't worry," she said. "You and Kevin will do great."

"Thanks. Oh, and about Kevin—we went to Downtown D'Lights together. I mean, I thought it was a date, but the whole thing was a disaster. And now he thinks I like Pete."

"Pete?"

"Mr. Sugarman's grandson. He moved here this year. He's in my math class. Anyway, I'm trying to figure out how to get things back on track with Kevin."

"Sash, I think you should talk to Kevin, tell him how you feel."

"But how?" I thought about the ideas I'd found on the Internet. "Should I text him?"

"No."

"Write him a note?"

"No, Sash. You need to *talk* to Kevin. This isn't just about how *you* feel. It's about his feelings too."

Talk to him? I talked to Kevin all the time—we joked around, we talked about dance and school—but this was different. This was hard. I couldn't imagine telling him I liked him. I needed another plan—something cute, something clever, something that didn't involve me standing in front of him baring my soul.

Before I parked my phone on the kitchen counter for the night, I scrolled through the texts Karly had sent me. I hadn't responded to any of them, and I certainly wasn't going to call her. She'd given up on our dream. She traded it in for Quiz Bowl and Ahmed and Tech Magnet. Worst of all, she'd traded me in too.

All morning at school, I dreaded lunch. Ms. Kumar had called a meeting. That meant Kevin, Ryan, Mira, and Anna would have plenty of opportunity to tease me about Petasha. I didn't want Pete to catch on, and I really didn't want the rumor to spread.

On the way to the meeting, I caught up with Anna and Mira.

"Where's Pete?" Anna asked.

"About that." I took a deep breath. "Can you stop with the whole Petasha thing?"

"What? Do you like Sashete better?"

"No. I don't like any of it. I don't like Pete."

"I told you." Mira stopped walking and faced Anna, then me. "I told her you didn't like Pete."

"You don't? Really, Sash?" Anna said. "But he's so cute, in a shy, sweet, new kid in town sort of way. And I knew you had a crush on someone, so I assumed . . ."

"You did make that Google doc," Mira said. "It was so adorkable."

"Great. I'm glad I entertain you." I kept walking. "That's what friends are for, right? Entertainment?"

"No, Sash. Of course not." Anna caught up to me. "But *who* do you like?"

"Seriously? Do you honestly think I would tell you two?"

"I bet it's Ryan." Mira was on my other side.

"Good luck with that," Anna said as we walked into Ms. Kumar's classroom.

"No. It's not Ryan," I said, my voice getting loud.

"What about Ryan?" Kevin asked, putting down his sandwich.

"Nothing," I said. "Absolutely nothing."

"You sure?" Kevin raised one eyebrow and then the other, alternating them until I started to laugh.

"Yeah, I'm sure." I wanted to sit down next to him, but another kid was already in that spot. I glanced over at Pete. There was an open seat next to him, but that didn't seem like a good move. I may have cleared up the whole Petasha thing with Anna and Mira, but Kevin still didn't know the truth. I sat down next to another girl. When Ryan came in, he sat down next to Pete.

Once everyone was there, Ms. Kumar ran through what needed to be done. She congratulated Pete and me on our publicity so far, and she encouraged everyone to take to social media.

"We want to sell a lot of tickets. We have a great cause." She smiled at me. "And we want to raise a lot of money. Also, the decorations are coming along, but Kevin and Ryan need your help this week. On the days you're not signed up for a lunchtime rehearsal slot, I expect you to be in the art room working. Understand?"

Most kids nodded; some said okay. I was glad because it gave me something to do other than stand around and look for a place to sit in the cafeteria.

"We only have eight days until the dress rehearsal. Nine days before the show. I know you are all working hard. There have been a couple of changes with some of the acts, and unfortunately we've had one person drop out."

Thanks a lot, Karly.

"This is not supposed to be a high stakes, stressful event." Ms. Kumar sat down on her desk. "I want to make sure we keep the focus on having fun and work-ing as a team." She crossed her legs. "Not on viewing each other as competition."

I raised my hand.

"Sasha?"

"Is the Summer Academy director still going to be the judge?"

"Yes. That's the plan." Ms. Kumar picked up a gift bag that was sitting next to her on the desk. "As I was saying, I want all of you to have fun and embrace the spirit of giving. So . . ." She shook the bag in her hand. "We're going to do Secret Snowman. You'll each pick a name out of the bag and then you'll leave notes, maybe treats, or an inexpensive gift for that person a few times during the week. And I mean inexpensive. Think homemade or the dollar bin at Target, not iTunes gift cards."

I hadn't done a secret gift exchange since the third grade, when the person who had me forgot to get me anything, so the teacher gave me a granola bar that had been sitting in her desk drawer for two months. But still, it had been fun. I had baked cookies and thought up elaborate clues for my secret person.

"The reveal will be after the show, during the reception." Ms. Kumar nodded at me. "Speaking of the reception, Sasha, we need to talk about the refreshments. Did you receive the email with the names of students who are willing to bake?"

"Um, yes," I said. Hadn't I? I was still thinking about Secret Snowman, wondering who would pick me.

Ms. Kumar walked around the room, holding out the bag. One by one, the kids reached in and pulled out a slip of paper. When Kevin picked his, I watched, and as he silently read the name, his face broke into a wide smile. Could it be me?

When it was my turn, there were only three names

left. I closed my eyes and pulled out the first piece of paper I touched.

It was Kevin.

Yes! I knew instantly that that was the way I could tell him how I felt—my Secret Snowman gifts would be a series of hints that I liked him. And then, after the show, when it was time to reveal my identity, Kevin would know my secret.

It was a perfect plan.

Chapter Seventeen
THE POWER OF A STICKY NOTE

It was after eleven o'clock at night when I finished putting everything together: a mug filled with chocolate kisses; a box of Swedish fish with the note, "I'm hooked on you"; a one dollar bill where I'd written "You're the" and then circled the ONE with a Sharpie; a bottle of Orange Crush (not only was it Kevin's favorite soda, but *crush*, get it?). I'd even made a playlist on Spotify and a fake email address so I could send Kevin the link anonymously.

It was the perfect lineup of "Secret Snowman/I Like You" gifts.

Okay, so maybe the Swedish fish note was a little corny, and I may have included one too many love songs on the playlist, but I'd tried being subtle before and that didn't get me very far. Plus, Kevin appreciated over-the-top. I knew Kevin. He'd love it.

Getting into bed, I felt ready for the rest of the week. Even my science grade was back up to a 94—and I'd already started studying for next week's test. I was feeling good about everything.

Well, everything except Karly. I'd avoided her all day (including ducking into the library when she was headed toward me in the hall after third period). And I hadn't returned any of her texts or phone calls. She'd even tried to FaceTime me twice, but I ignored her.

Tomorrow, I told myself. I'd figure it out tomorrow.

But the next day, I was so busy I didn't have time to think about Karly.

That was until I opened my dance bag at JayJay's and found my first Secret Snowman gift. The red and white striped tissue paper reminded me of our Holidaze Spectacular costumes and inside was a really cute to-do list pad and a package of pencils. Each pencil had a different inspirational saying printed on it: YOU GOT THIS! YOU CAN DO IT! GO FOR IT! They were adorable! And they were just the sort of thing Karly and I would give to each other. I looked around, half expecting Karly to be standing there. Of course, I knew she couldn't have given them to me— she wasn't in the gift exchange, but maybe she had told Kevin to get them for me?

Oh, what was I going to do about Karly? I was still mad, but I also missed her. A lot. And it wasn't just since Sunday's blowup. We hadn't really been our BFF-selves since Thanksgiving. We used to tell each other everything, and share everything. Things had really changed.

When I arrived at the Hall's house to practice with Kevin that evening, Karly wasn't home yet. I couldn't figure out if I was disappointed or relieved. On the one hand, I wanted to see her. On the other hand, I didn't know what I would say. Every time I tried to let go of my anger, it popped right back up.

"Karly will be home for dinner." Mrs. Hall touched my hand (a total clue Karly had told her mom what had happened). "And I hope you'll stay."

"Okay. Thanks." Dinner at the Hall's always sounded good to me, and maybe this was the perfect way for Karly and I to make up.

In the basement, Kevin and I ran through the whole routine. The dancing was pretty tight, but with only the two of us, the singing was a lot harder. There were a bunch of seriously cringe-y spots.

"I think we should drop the singing," Kevin said. "The sound equipment is good in the auditorium. It'll sound better. Better than us."

"But—"

"You know," Kevin glanced over at the keyboard. "We could ask Karly to help. She could play the keyboard and sing. And we could focus on our awesome dancing."

"No. Absolutely not. She quit."

"Really?" Kevin gave me a funny look. "It sounded like you fired her."

"She was going to quit. I just beat her to it."

"You sure about that?"

"Yes." Though, actually, maybe Kevin was right. During our fight, I had sort of interrupted Karly mid-sentence.

Kevin shrugged. "Anyway, I bet she'd do it. And she does have the best voice out of the three of us." He flicked my arm. "Come on, think about it."

"I don't know." I knew it was a good idea, but . . .

"We can ask her at dinner tonight."

"Maybe."

When Kevin and I were done rehearsing, we headed upstairs. That's when Mrs. Hall told us Quiz Bowl practice was running late (surprise, surprise) and that Karly wouldn't be home for dinner after all. Mrs. Hall looked at me like she wanted to say, "I'm sorry."

I again felt disappointed and relieved at the same time. Being mad at your best friend was seriously confusing.

But dinner ended up being fun—it was hard not to have fun at the Hall's. Plus, I sat next to Kevin. He teased me about how he wanted his top hat back and how maybe I'd taken it because I wanted to wear it. Then he talked about what his Secret Snowman gave him. He sounded excited, which made me feel happy.

"You know who has me, don't you?" he asked in a way that made me think he might be guessing it was me.

"I'm not telling." I thought about what I'd received. "Do you know who has me?"

"Yup."

"Who?"

He gestured that he was locking his lips. "Not telling."

"Fine," I said, hoping it was him.

On Wednesday, I put the box of Swedish fish on Kevin's chair in math class.

On Thursday, I slipped a paper heart into his reading book, replacing the torn-up piece of paper he was using as a bookmark.

On Friday afternoon, I emailed him the playlist.

I was feeling really good about the whole thing. Every day, Kevin told me what he'd received from his Secret Snowman, even reading me my note on the Swedish fish and laughing like it was an inside joke between the two of us.

He knew it was me. I was sure of it.

Meanwhile my Secret Snowman (Kevin, I was pretty sure) was hard at work.

On Wednesday, he left me an awesome dance poster on the outside of my locker.

On Thursday, he sent me a playlist (only one love song). Most of the music was indie rock, songs I didn't know Kevin even liked (he was full of surprises). I kept shuffling the playlist, reading his feelings for me into each song. It wasn't easy: Turning "Supermarket Smash Up" into a love song was a challenge, but I did it.

On Friday, he left me a homemade bookmark. I found it after school when I was dumping out my backpack, trying to find my earbuds. The bookmark was a paper candy cane. Super cute! It reminded me of the candy cane appliqués we'd glued onto our costumes. It even smelled like peppermint.

Meanwhile, Karly continued to reach out to me. On Wednesday, she left a two-minute voice mail apology in which she recited a poem she'd written about our friendship called "My Bae" (I did crack a smile listening to it). On Thursday, she sent me a text: *Can we talk?*

I wanted to talk but . . . every time I was about to call her, I got angry all over again.

Then, on Friday afternoon, when I was rustling through my dance bag, still trying to find my earbuds, I found a yellow sticky note stuck to the bottom of my jazz shoes. It was one of Karly's Quiz Bowl questions. I read it and then I stuck it on my bulletin board, right next to a photograph of Karly and me from Halloween in fifth grade. There we were, standing side by side in matching white wigs and mustaches and lab coats. We both held up clipboards where we'd written formulas and famous Albert Einstein quotes. I'd forgotten that back then we both wanted to be scientists just as much as we wanted to be dancers.

"I'm going to pick up a pizza for dinner." Mom peeked her head into my room. "Do you want a side salad too?"

"Sure." I turned away from the bulletin board. "Thanks."

When Mom left, I did some stretches and then once I was warmed up, I practiced my leaps. I didn't know how long I had before our downstairs neighbor started hitting the ceiling with her broom, but I needed to take my chances. I wanted to get some more height on the calypso and the only way I'd get it is if I practiced. Over and over again, I worked through the steps: first position, tendu, tombé, right leg kicks up, left leg up, arching back . . .

I worked on it until Mom came home. Yay! I'd made it through an entire practice without our downstairs neighbor complaining. I wasn't sure if I was learning to land quieter or if our neighbor was out, but it didn't matter; my calypso leap was feeling better, much better. And so was I.

We ate at the kitchen counter. (We did everything at the dining room table except actually eat.)

"I ran into Mrs. Hall at Salvatore's," Mom said as she blotted the grease off a piece of pizza with a paper towel. "You didn't tell me Karly was competing in the televised Quiz Bowl tournament. That's so exciting!"

"Yeah," I said, thinking about another text I'd ignored—one from Mira and Anna asking if I wanted to get a ride from Anna's mom to the tournament the next morning. They'd even texted me a photo of the sign they'd made that said GO KARLY!

"Mrs. Hall said you can get a ride with them, but they're leaving pretty early."

I chewed my pizza slowly, focusing on the flavor.

"Sasha, you are going, right? I know you're still upset, but Karly is your best friend."

I swallowed, then said, "I'll think about it." But I'd already made up my mind.

After dinner, back in my room, I took the yellow sticky note off my bulletin board. I was pretty sure Karly knew the answer, but still . . . I pulled out my phone and texted her the question: *What country hasn't been in a war since 1847?*

She responded right away: *SASHA!* And a string of hearts and my favorite dancer emoji.

I smiled wide as I called her.

"Wrong," I said when Karly answered. "The correct answer is Switzerland!" And we both laughed and laughed. It felt good to be a best friend again.

chapter Eighteen

ONE STEP FORWARD, TWO STEPS BACK

The auditorium was packed, but Anna, Mira, and I had arrived early enough to score seats in the third row. We were decked out in our school colors, red and blue, and I'd even put a ridiculously big red bow in my hair (saved from fifth grade when Karly and I used to wear them for real). Mira brought pom-poms for us to cheer with, and when the television camera swept over our section, we went wild.

When Karly came onto the stage, I was so nervous that I grabbed Mira's and Anna's hands and squeezed them tight. But Karly didn't look nervous. And when it was her turn to introduce herself, she smiled and sounded confident.

"Look at her," Anna whispered in my ear.

"I'm so proud," Mira said, sounding more like a mom than a friend, but to be honest, I felt the exact same way.

Mrs. Hall, who was sitting in the row in front of us (next to Kevin and Mr. Hall), turned around and winked at me, and I smiled back. I knew how hard Karly had worked for this moment, and now it was here!

In the first round of toss-up questions, Karly buzzed in three times with two correct answers. Yay! During the bonus questions, the team had five seconds to confer, but it seemed like a lot longer to me. My palms were sweating as the team whispered. I noticed Karly and Ahmed's heads touched as they discussed the answer, which Ahmed gave—correctly!

I smiled. *They go well together*, I thought.

The competition continued until the two teams were tied before the final question:

Edelweiss is the national flower of what two countries?

Karly buzzed.

"Austria and . . ."

I held my breath. My heart pounded.

"Switzerland," she said.

I stood up to cheer; Mira and Anna and I all hugged as the host announced our team as the winners.

"We did it!" Mira yelled.

Outside the auditorium, we waited in the lobby while Karly and the team took photos. Mrs. Hall was clicking away and Kevin was hamming it up behind her, making sure everyone on the team was smiling, if not cracking up, in every photo.

When Karly was finished, she walked over to us.

"Thanks for coming, you guys. It means a lot to me."

"You were so awesome!" I said, and gave her a big hug.

"I knew you would win it," Mira said. "I just knew it."

Anna opened up her arms wide and said, "Group hug!" The four of us fell into each other, swaying from side to side and laughing. It was the best feeling.

In the afternoon, I headed over to Sugarman's to meet up with Pete before going to the Hall's to rehearse with Kevin. Pete and I needed to review the promo video one more time before we uploaded it. But when I entered the market, I didn't see him.

"Is Pete here?" I asked Mr. Sugarman, who was wiping down the counter in the back. I was pretty sure he didn't have a basketball game until later, but maybe he was at practice. I hoped not.

"Uh . . ." Mr. Sugarman hesitated. "Yes." Then he turned toward the storage room in the back. "Pete! Sasha's here."

A few seconds later, Pete appeared. He stuffed something into his pocket and then headed over to me.

"Is this an okay time?" I asked.

"Yeah, it's good."

"Great." I dropped my dance bag down next to one of the tables, and Pete brought over his computer.

"I changed the beginning a little." He pressed PLAY. "But everything else is pretty much what we came up with last time."

I watched, blushing at the opening clip. It was a shot of me, standing outside the door of the auditorium, opening the door and saying, "Follow me!" I didn't even remember him filming it.

When the video finished, Pete asked, "What'd you think?"

"I love it!" I said. It was really good. "The only thing I would change is the end—we should do a close-up of the flyer to make sure people can see the details: date, time, and place."

We chatted about school while Pete figured out how to zoom in. "Okay, what do you think?" He turned toward me. "Is that close enough?"

"Perfect," I said. "Let's upload it." Thanks to a friend of Ms. Kumar's, our video was going up on a couple of local sites, and it was also going to air on our cable station.

As Pete sent the link to Ms. Kumar, I started humming "Supermarket Smash Up," one of the songs my Secret Snowman (Kevin, I was sure) had put on his playlist for me.

"That's a good tune." Pete leaned back in the chair.

"You know it?"

"Know it? They're like my favorite band."

"The song was on the playlist my Secret Snowman made. I like it!"

"Your Secret Snowman must really like you."

"You think?" I smiled. "I hope so."

Pete smiled back at me, and I felt my cheeks heat up.

"So, what have you gotten from yours?" I asked.

"A pack of gum."

"That's it?"

"Yeah." Pete shrugged. "It's no big deal.

No big deal? It might not be for him, but for me, it sure was. A lot (everything!) was riding on Secret Snowman.

I glanced at the clock and realized how much time had passed. "Oh! I need to head out now." I stood up to go, and Pete looked surprised.

"Dance practice. We only have a few more days."

"Ah. By the way, when I was dropping cookies off at the Senior Center this morning, Big T gave me the mittens and hats they made for the tree. I'll bring them to school Monday."

"Thanks!" I swung my bag onto my shoulder and waved goodbye. I was surprised how disappointed I felt to be leaving. Usually, dance was what I wanted to be doing most.

Kevin and I only had a few practices left before the dress rehearsal and I was, well, starting to freak out a little. Was our dance good enough? Were *we* good enough?

And as soon as I reached the Hall's basement, I had a bigger freak out. Ryan was standing next to Kevin.

"Sa-sha!" Kevin said my name as if he were saying ta-da.

"Hey." I turned to Ryan and nodded. "What's up?"

I was trying to stay calm but really I was thinking: *What—I mean*, what—*was Ryan doing practicing in the Hall's basement?* This was our space. And even though Kevin might be popping into Ryan's act to do a couple of acro moves, this was a competition. Ryan was one of our biggest competitors.

"We learned this really cool move in the acro workshop," Kevin said. "We've been practicing it a lot, and I was thinking we could use it as the finale in our act."

I swallowed hard. "You mean Ryan's act?"

"No. Ours."

"What?" I took a step back. "We *have* an ending. We choreographed it days ago."

"Sash, just listen. You know how we've been thinking the ending could use a little something extra—well, Ryan will just pop in at the end. You know, a cameo, like I'm doing in his."

"No." I took a step back. "Our ending is great."

Great was an overstatement, but Ryan was *not* going to be part of our routine.

"It's good, but what if we could make it even better? You're the one who's always pushing us to be better."

"Are you kidding me?" I looked at Kevin and what I saw then was not the boy I'd decided to have a crush on, but the Kevin I'd known since third grade—burping, messy, too loud Kevin. "We're *not* changing our routine three days before the show." *Plus*, I wanted to scream, *Ryan isn't even in our act!*

"I'm gonna go," Ryan said.

"But . . ." Kevin started to say something else, but he stopped.

"Later, dude." Ryan headed toward the stairs. "Bye, Sasha."

I dropped my dance bag on the basement floor and turned toward Kevin. "You know this is a competition, right? Only one act wins. Don't you want it to be us? If we win, we'll be dancing at the Summer Academy this summer. Just like we dreamed."

"Yeah, but—"

"But what?"

"Forget it."

Our rehearsal did not go well. Kevin bumped into

me a couple of times and my singing sounded super pitchy. It was only three days before the show, and we were falling apart. And because of what Kevin had said, I felt totally insecure about the ending. He was right. It could be stronger. But how?

"Wait," Kevin called from the stairs when I was leaving. "You forgot your bag." He swung it toward me.

"Thanks," I said, but it came out angry. I was angry.

On the walk home, I started getting outraged again that Kevin wanted Ryan to do an acro move in our act. It was *our* act. Just the two of us. Ryan didn't belong in it.

Why was it that just when Karly and I were back on track, everything else that mattered (our routine, Kevasha) was falling apart?

Inside the apartment, I kicked off my boots.

"Are we even getting a tree this year?" I asked Mom as she poured boiling water from the kettle into her mug.

"Of course we are." She dipped her teabag into the water.

"When?"

"I thought we'd get it this weekend. Claire will be home, and we'll both be done with school."

I glanced around the living room; there wasn't a single Christmas decoration up, but there was an unopened moving box in the corner (still).

"Do we even have our stockings?" I headed toward my room. "Or did you throw those away?"

"Sasha!"

"You didn't even buy a chocolate advent calendar this year. You always used to do that."

I closed my bedroom door hard, not waiting for Mom to answer.

Anyway, there was nothing she could say that would make me feel better. It wasn't just the bad rehearsal and Mom's lack of holiday spirit that was stressing me out. I had five days and a lot to do: end of the semester tests in almost every subject, wrapping up the hat and mitten drive, doing a final push on social media to promote the show, and organizing the refreshments for the reception, which I kept putting off. And the holiday gift exchange . . .

My mind whirled with everything I needed to accomplish in the next one hundred and twenty hours. I needed some music.

I unzipped my dance bag and dug around for my earbuds. But instead I found a wrapped gift with a note that said "From your Secret Snowman." That was a surprise! Kevin must've slipped it in when I'd forgotten my bag in the Hall's basement. My salty mood started to dissolve.

I unwrapped it: It was a mug with a packet of hot chocolate and a candy cane inside. Peppermint cocoa! My Secret Snowman knew exactly what I needed.

Chapter Nineteen
MISTAKES

When I arrived at school on Monday, Pete was already there in the front hall, hanging the hats and mittens from the Senior Center on the tree.

"Thank you!" I dropped my backpack and pulled a hat out of the box. "Wow!"

"I know," Pete said. "They made a lot." He stepped back. "The tree's almost full."

"This is great." I hung a hat on a high branch. "And the Knitting Club said they'd be done with theirs tomorrow!" I felt good that the tree was coming together and we'd have a lot to donate.

"Excellent job," Ms. Medley said as she passed by us.

When we were finished, Pete and I walked to math class together. We didn't say much, but it wasn't awkward either.

Outside the classroom, he stopped. "Are you going to the art room at lunch today?"

"Yeah."

"Me too," Pete said. As he smiled, I noticed he had a slight dimple on his right cheek. How had I not seen that before?

All morning, I tried to figure out how to give Kevin his next present—the Orange Crush soda. I'd put it in a brown paper bag with his name on it (writing with my left hand to disguise my handwriting). It had been hidden in my backpack, going with me from class to class.

At lunch, I arrived in the art room before anyone else. I put the brown bag on the long table where a bunch of the finished snowflakes were waiting to be strung with fishing line. Then I went to the bathroom. When I came back, Anna, Mira, and Karly were standing at another table, already working.

Kevin and Ryan were the last two to arrive.

"Typical," Mira said. "They think the rest of us are going to do all the work while they goof off."

"Boys," Anna muttered. But I just watched Kevin as he walked to the back table.

"Look, Kev." Ryan pointed to the brown paper bag. "For you."

"I'm going to wash my hands," I said to my group as I headed toward the sink in the back of the room. I wanted to get a better view of Kevin's reaction when he saw the bottle of Crush and got it—the double meaning of the gift.

He picked up the bag and peeked inside. "Awesome." He pulled out the orange soda. "It's my favorite!" Grinning, he glanced over at Ryan.

Then Kevin unscrewed the cap, and the orange soda exploded, spraying all over him and the table in front of him—including the finished snowflakes on it.

"Oh no!" I lurched forward, but the damage was already done.

"Whoa." He wiped his face with his shirt.

"Here," Ryan said, grabbing a bunch of paper towels.

"The snowflakes!" Kevin picked up a soggy one. "They've melted."

I started mopping up the floor with the cloth Ms. McMann handed me. I felt terrible. It would take hours to remake the ones coated in soda. And it was my fault. The bottle of soda had been bumping around in my backpack all morning. No wonder it exploded.

"We can save them," Ryan said as he blotted one with a paper towel—but all the glued-on glitter came off. "Okay, maybe not." He held the snowflake up and orange soda dripped onto my neck. Yuck. I wiped it off and stood up.

"Orange-tinted snowflakes!" Kevin joked. "I like them, they're kinda sci-fi."

How could he be joking about this? It was a disaster.

I didn't get home until seven-thirty that night. A bunch of us had stayed after school remaking the snowflakes, and then Kevin and I practiced at the Hall's house, which took an extra-long time because Kevin kept clutching his throat, saying it was sore. I told him it was his nerves, because there was *no way* Kevin was getting sick. The show was in three days!

Then I got home, and Mom lectured me about how exhausted I must be (like I needed her to point that out).

"I'll be glad when this show is behind you."

"Thanks, Mom. That's real supportive."

"I am supportive, Sasha, but this has taken up all your time—I want you to do other things too."

"Like robotics," I muttered. "No thank you."

I studied in my room that night, staying up late to review for the two tests I had the next day. Right before I went to bed, I pulled out the to-do list pad my Secret Snowman had given me and picked up one of the cute pencils. I wrote down what I needed to get done the next day. I reread the list, feeling like I was forgetting something, but it was late, and I was tired, and . . .

I lifted up the pencil and read the words printed along the side: YOU GOT THIS!

I smiled. "You got this!" I said aloud.

"Sash, you can't do everything," Karly said to me after school the next day.

"I know." I opened the door to the auditorium. "It's just, I think they could use our help."

"Thirty minutes. That's it. I need to rewrite my social studies essay."

An hour later, I stood on a ladder as Pete handed up a snowflake.

"You got it?" he asked.

"Yup." Reaching up, I taped the fishing wire to the ceiling; my legs shook. The snowflake spun, sparkling under the light.

"Looks good." Pete handed me another one.

I glanced over at Ryan and Kevin, who were goofing off on a ladder on the other side of the auditorium.

"Focus," Karly yelled at them. "You need to redo that one." She pointed to a snowflake that was hanging too low.

It took us almost two hours to decorate, and then I convinced Karly to wait while Kevin and I did a quick run-through of our routine (dancing only). I wanted Kevin to save his voice. Our ending looked sloppy—it still wasn't right, but I didn't know how to fix it.

"Don't worry," Karly said from the second row. "A bad dress rehearsal usually means an excellent performance."

"Yeah, but this isn't the dress rehearsal. Tomorrow is." I rubbed my face. "This is bad." I looked over at Kevin. "I think we're getting worse."

"It's okay, Sasha." He pulled a dollar bill out of his pocket and held it out for me to see. It was the dollar bill I'd given him, the one I'd marked "You're the One." "I think I know who my Secret Snowman is." He smiled.

"You do?" I smiled back at him.

"Yeah," he said softly, almost dreamily, as if his heart was melting.

He knew it was me. I was sure of it.

"Sasha." Karly stood between us, putting on her coat. "Anna just texted me. She wants to know if you still need her to bake something for the reception?"

My heart dropped. That's what had I forgotten to do. The refreshments!

"One hundred and twenty cookies?" Mom said as Karly and I lined up the ingredients on the kitchen counter. "You can't make that many cookies tonight. We can buy them."

"No. We have to bake them." I opened the lid on the canister of flour. "People are willing to pay more money for homemade."

"Well then, other kids should be making them, too. You girls shouldn't be the only ones doing this." Mom shook her head.

"I know." I started pouring the dry ingredients

into the largest bowl we owned. Mom was right. And if I'd sent out the reminder email when I should have, we would've had more help. What a fail.

"Stop." Karly nudged my hand. "That's enough flour."

I put down the measuring cup, realizing I'd forgotten to keep count. I picked up the salt. It poured quickly onto the tablespoon, overflowing and spilling into the bowl.

"Let me know if you need anything else." Mom grabbed a few books and headed to her room.

"Sash, you seriously look like you're going to fall asleep." Karly lined a baking sheet with parchment paper. "Did you sleep last night?"

"Yes," I said, closing my eyes for just a second. "I think I forgot the salt. Did you add it?"

"Nope."

An hour and a half later, with a spatula in one hand and an oven mitt in the other, Karly transferred the last batch of cookies onto the wire drying rack.

"We should try one," she said.

"Go ahead." I lifted my head up from the counter and yawned.

As soon as she bit into it, her face scrunched up.

"Yuck." She dropped the cookie. "Did you add the sugar?"

"What? No . . . I thought you did . . ."

Both of us looked over at the full bag of sugar sitting on the counter. Oh no.

I took a bite of the cookie too—or, should I say, the high-sodium dog biscuit. Blech. Even a dog wouldn't eat that. I wanted to cry. We'd just spent two hours making one hundred and twenty inedible cookies.

"What are we going to do? We're out of flour." I glanced over at the empty carton. "And eggs. I can't believe this. We'll have to go to the store."

On the way over to Sugarman's Market, Karly said, "Sash, I think we should buy the cookies."

"No." I was determined to raise the most amount of money possible for the meals program at the Senior Center. And store-bought cookies wouldn't cut it.

"But I have to go home and finish my essay. It's due tomorrow." We turned onto Main Street.

"Okay." We passed by Salvatore's; the color lights on its fake Christmas tree in the window flashed. "I can make the cookies."

"But you can't, not by yourself."

"It'll be fine." I opened the door to Sugarman's and the bells jangled much too merrily for my mood.

I grabbed the largest bag of flour they had. "What do you think?" I turned around to ask Karly, but she wasn't there. *It should be enough*, I thought as I headed over to the refrigerator for eggs.

"Karly?" Where was she? I couldn't carry everything. "Karly!"

"Here I am." Karly stood at the end of the aisle; Pete was next to her.

He smiled. "Hey, Sasha."

I hesitated. "Hey." I looked at Karly with a what's-going-on expression.

She took a step toward me. "Before you say no, I've already talked to Mr. Sugarman, and he said yes."

"What're you talking about?"

"We're going to make the cookies here." Pete handed me an apron. "We've got a commercial mixer, multiple ovens—"

"But . . ."

"I insist," Mr. Sugarman said as he appeared on the other side of me. "All you need is a hairnet and you can get started." He nodded toward the prep area behind the counter.

Karly gave me a hug. "I'm sorry I have to leave." She looked over at Pete. "Have fun."

Within minutes, we were in the kitchen and my hands were washed, my apron was on, and my hair was in a net. (Pete had super short hair, but he put a hairnet on too.) We added all the ingredients, this time very carefully following the recipe. After we mixed in the eggs, Pete asked if I wanted to blend some crushed candy cane into half the batter.

"That's a good idea!" I said. He went to get the candy canes and I noticed his shoes had flour dusting the toes. There was something so sweet about his messy shoes.

"Here you go." Pete handed me a rolling pin and a plastic bag filled with candy canes, and we got to work crushing them. I started humming "Winter Dreams."

"That's the song you guys are doing for your act, right?"

"Yeah. 'Winter Dreams.'"

"You're going to do great," Pete said.

"I hope so. I really want to win the scholarship."

I liked spending time with Pete. When I was with him, I could still hear myself think, which was so different from when I was with Kevin.

As I pressed cookie cutters into the dough, my mind wandered to the ending of our routine, and then an idea started to form for the perfect finish.

By the time Mom picked me up, the cookies were baked and stored. Thank you, Pete Sugarman! And I'd come up with a new ending for our routine. It was a little bit romantic, and the perfect way for Kevin and I to reveal our crushes on each other. Kevasha was back on track.

Chapter Twenty
Stage Frights and Fights

The next morning when I sat down in math, Kevin whispered in a raspy voice, "What's up?" At first, I thought he was joking around, but then I saw the cough drop in his mouth.

"I thought you were getting better!"

"I actually feel better, but I can't really talk."

My heart sank. How was Kevin going to sing? "But the dress rehearsal's tonight. The *show* is tomorrow!"

"I know. And I've got these." He tapped a jumbo box of generic cough drops on the desk. "Don't worry."

But I was worried. I also wondered if I should explain the change I was going to make to the ending, but I decided I'd surprise him at the dress rehearsal.

It was definitely the sort of thing he could improvise. I mean, considering he liked me, it wouldn't be hard.

By the time we met up for the dress rehearsal in the auditorium, Kevin sounded like a croaking frog.

"I'll be fine dancing." He wore the red morph suit. "But I can't . . "

"Sing." Karly stood next to him. "I can," she said.

"You sure?"

"I'm sure."

I hugged her, crushing my tutu between us.

The three of us waited backstage; we listened to the clarinet players and the lip-synchers. We couldn't see the jugglers, but we did hear a couple of balls drop. We watched from the wings for Mira and then Anna; they both slayed it. Ryan was the act before us, so Kevin left to do his acro moves, but I didn't watch Ryan's performance on purpose. Ryan was probably our biggest competition and the fact that Kevin was helping him still annoyed me.

We were the last act—the finale—and that made me feel good. The Holidaze Spectacular always ended with one of the strongest acts, and I wondered if Ms. Kumar thought we were going to win. At the very least, she must've thought we had a chance.

With Karly at the keyboard, Kevin and I took our places on the stage. The music started: one, two, three, four, five, six, seven, eight . . . Every step was synched up, every move was tight—we were on point.

Kevin moved into our finishing pose—both of us were supposed to take a knee with our arms reaching up and back, but as Kevin kneeled, I stayed standing and then did two turns toward him.

Startled, he caught my eye as if to say, What are you doing?

I smiled wider, as I sat down on his knee. I leaned forward—my plan was to kiss his cheek, a tiny peck, but Kevin jerked his head back before I could reach him.

"Whoa, Sash." Kevin stood up, bumping me off his knee.

Karly stopped playing.

I heard laughter coming from the audience. I looked down. Everyone—all the other performers, and Ms. Kumar—stared at us.

"What was that?" Kevin sounded mad.

"Our new ending. I thought you'd like it."

He wiped his cheek where I'd tried to kiss it. "Yeah, no, that's not going to work."

More laughter sounded from the audience.

"Sasha and Kevin, why don't you two take a moment." Ms. Kumar pointed toward backstage. "And everyone else, I need your attention." She sat down at the edge of the stage. "We need to go over some final details."

"But why not?" I whispered to Kevin as we walked backstage. "I thought you wanted me to kiss you."

"Wait, what?" He shook his head. "Why? Why would I want you to kiss me?"

"Because you like me," I whispered. "You did all these things, like teasing and trying to make me laugh, things I thought meant . . ." I looked down at my tutu; one of the candy cane appliqués had fallen off.

"Sash. You know you're my best friend, but I don't like you, not like that."

I felt dizzy, as if everything around me was shifting. He didn't have a crush on me? *Kevasha* was crumbling and I was trying to find something I could hold on to. "But this whole time with the gifts. You knew I was your Secret Snowman, and you liked it."

"Uh, no." His face reddened. "I didn't know." Kevin ran his hand through his hair. "I thought it was Ryan."

"Ryan? Why would you want Ryan to be your Secret Snowman?" As soon as I said it out loud I knew the answer, but it didn't make sense.

"I like Ryan." He leaned against the wall.

"But . . ."

"Sash. I'm gay."

My stomach dropped. "You're gay? What . . . Why didn't you tell me?"

"I don't know. Everything's kind of confusing. Ryan's my first, like, real person crush, and I wasn't sure—"

"But you should've told me. I'm your best friend." I saw another candy cane appliqué that had dropped onto the ground. "Was," I said quietly. "I was your best friend."

"Sasha." Kevin reached toward me, but I turned and ran out of the auditorium.

Chapter Twenty-One
FAILURE

Outside, the wind blew hard and the snow pelted my face as I started walking toward home. I pulled my hat out of my pocket—it was the one Miss Melinda had given me, the one I'd worn to Downtown D'Lights Night. I shuddered, remembering my failed first date with Kevin. It wasn't a date. At least, not for Kevin and me. I thought of Kevin and Ryan skating together on the ice and the pictures on Instagram. I should've known. My mind flashed forward to what had just happened on the stage. I was so embarrassed. How was I ever going to face everyone again?

I pulled the hat low over my ears, wishing I could pull it over my whole face. I wanted to disappear.

Tears ran down my cheek, and I rubbed them away with my mitten. How could I be so stupid? While I'd been busy checking off clues and coming up with ways to tell Kevin I liked him, I hadn't seen what was really happening—that Kevin and Ryan liked each other.

I kept my head down. Everything was quiet except the crunch of my boots on the snowy sidewalk and the swishing sound of cars driving past me. It was dark except for their headlights and the occasional streetlamp.

Two blocks away from school, I heard a car pull up next to me.

"Sasha!" Mom called through the rolled-down window.

I climbed over the snow bank and opened the door.

"Hi," she said.

I slid into the seat next to her. Heat blasted from the vents. I pulled off my hat.

"Karly called. She said you were walking home."

Nodding, I stretched the seatbelt over my coat and buckled.

"You should've called me."

"Can we just go home?" As soon as I said the word home, I started to cry.

Mom didn't start driving. She reached for a tissue from her stash in the glove compartment. "Sasha, what's going on? Is this about your grades?"

I snatched the tissue from her hand. "No, this isn't about my grades." I wiped my face.

"Is it about the apartment? I promise it will start to feel more like home." She reached out to touch my knee, but my body jerked away before she could reach me. "What is it? I can't fix it if you don't tell me."

"You can't fix this." Snow hit the windshield and turned to slush.

"Maybe not." Mom turned on the windshield wipers. "But sometimes talking about it makes you feel better."

I didn't want to talk. Not to Mom. Not to anyone.

"Why don't you take a hot bath?" Mom suggested as we stepped inside the apartment.

I pulled off my boots and stuck them in the tray by the door. "Okay."

She took my coat and hung it up. My phone was in its pocket, but the last thing I wanted to do was look at it. What if someone had videoed the ending of our routine and posted it on Instagram? I shivered.

"A bath is just what you need." Mom handed me a small bag. "This was going to be a stocking stuffer, but I think you could use it now."

As I opened the bag, the scent of sweet vanilla escaped. Inside was a bath bomb.

"Did you see how cute it is?"

I pulled out the package—it was actually three bath bombs, forming a snowman. "Yeah." It was super cute, but I couldn't get myself to say it.

As I ran the water, I watched the bath bomb dissolve, breaking down into little bits until only tiny grains were left. In the tub, I sunk down low under the warm water. The scent of vanilla made me think of the sugar cookies Pete and I had baked. At least those would be a success.

Back in my room, Mom had laid out my fleece pajamas—my favorite ones. I put them on and flopped onto the bed, staring into space.

"Can I get you something to eat?" Mom asked, popping her head into my room. "A hot cocoa?"

"Nah. I'm good."

When Mom closed the door, my eyes drifted over to the top of my bookshelf. There was Kevin's top hat, the one Ryan had given to him. The one I'd basically stolen.

I grabbed my pillow and buried my head in it. I should've known. I should've known a lot of things.

True, I was angry Kevin hadn't told me he liked Ryan (or boys, in general). But mostly, I was angry with myself. Angry that I'd turned Kevasha into some sort of school project where I wouldn't stop until I got a one hundred. I'd chosen Kevin not because I had romantic feelings for him, but because when Karly said she had a crush, I thought I needed to have one too.

And Kevin seemed like the obvious answer. Never once did I actually think about feelings—Kevin's or mine.

I lay down and closed my eyes. I didn't want to think about it anymore.

Chapter Twenty-Two
A SNOW DAY

In the morning, Mom woke me up.

"Sasha." She handed me the phone. "It's Claire. She wants to talk to you."

"Hello," I said, my voice groggy. "Where are you?"

"California—but don't worry, I'll be home tonight."

At the window, Mom opened the blinds. I squinted. Everything outside was bright and white and blowing. What time was it?

"You have a snow day today!" Mom said. "Ms. Kumar sent an email saying she's trying to reschedule the show for Friday night."

I sat up.

"Don't worry," Claire said. "I'm not missing the show!"

"Okay." I was glad the show wasn't cancelled. Yes, dancing with Kevin would be awkward, but we'd worked so hard, and our dance was really good. Our costumes were super cute. I wanted the chance to perform, and maybe to win. Plus, the Senior Center was counting on us. "I can't wait for you to get here."

Mom gently pulled the door shut as she slipped out of my room.

"Me neither." Claire paused. "So Sash, what's going on?"

"Did Mom tell you to call me?"

"Yeah. She's worried. She thinks she's putting too much pressure on you. Are you stressed about Mom wanting you to apply to Tech Magnet?"

"I mean yes, sort of, but that's not why I'm upset."

"What is it?"

"It's Kevin." I sunk my head back on the pillow.

"Did you talk to him?"

"Talk? Not really, but I did try to show him how I felt." I cringed, thinking about my ridiculous Secret Snowman gifts and my attempt to kiss him on stage.

"Basically, I made a total fool of myself. And then he told me he liked Ryan."

"Ryan? Hmm. Do I know him?"

I sat up. "He's an eighth grader. He was in the show last year. Remember the illusionist?"

"Oh, yeah. He was awesome."

"Well, Kevin thinks so too. I can't believe Kevin's gay, and I didn't even know it."

"Okay. Kevin's gay." Claire did not sound surprised. "So now you know. What'd you say when Kevin told you?"

"Say? Not much . . . I kind of ran off."

"You ran off?"

"What was I supposed to do?"

"Sash," Claire said. "I'm sorry this didn't go the way you wanted. But what Kevin told you isn't about you. It's about him. He shared something really important with you, about who he is. That's not easy."

"Yeah, well, what I did wasn't easy either."

"I know."

"What should I do now?"

"I think Kevin needs his best friend."

Claire was right. But I didn't know how to make that happen, and this time, I wasn't going to Google it.

After our call, I took a deep breath and scrolled through my phone notifications. There were a string of texts from Karly, telling me to call her. There was a message from Pete: *You okay?*

As I slid my finger across the screen, I read the last text. It was from Kevin. No words. No emojis. Only a question mark.

I thought about what Claire said. Running off when your best friend tells you he's gay wasn't the smoothest move.

Bracing myself, I scrolled through my feed on Instagram. There were the usual selfies and a bunch of Snow Day memes, but there was nothing about my failed kiss. On Anna's insta, there was a photo from the dress rehearsal.

#WishUsLuckWeNeedIt #WorstRehearsalEver.

That was it.

#Relieved.

By noon, the snow had stopped and the sky was starting to clear, and I had an idea. It wasn't some big elaborate plan. There weren't a list of clues or cheesy gifts. It was simple, but I hoped more than anything it would get Kevin and me back into the friend zone— the best friend zone.

"Do you know where my snow pants are?" I asked Mom, who was at the table, wrapping a gift. She'd taken her last exam the day before and she already seemed more relaxed.

"Check in my closet. There's a box marked WINTER."

A few minutes later when I swished back into the living room, Mom said the streets were plowed and Claire's flight was scheduled to take off soon.

"I'm going to leave for the airport in a couple of hours. You want to come with me?"

"Yes, but first I need to do something."

"Go!" Mom shooed me toward the door. On the way out, I grabbed the bag where I'd put the things I needed.

Outside, everything was sparkling and white. Neighbors shoveled their driveways and sidewalks. I climbed over a massive snow bank to cross Main Street. When the sun broke through the clouds, I tilted my head toward the sky, where a swatch of deep blue appeared.

Outside Sugarman's, I spotted Pete shoveling the sidewalk. I walked faster, my heart beating quicker.

"Hey." He leaned on the shovel. "Did you hear the show's been rescheduled for tomorrow?"

"Yeah," I said. "You think our cookies are going to be okay?"

"No problem. I'll take them out of the freezer tomorrow morning."

"Thanks! I'm worried people aren't going to know that the show is rescheduled, though."

Pete pointed to a poster on the door of Sugarman's:

RESCHEDULED!
The Holidaze Spectacular
WILL BE
Friday, December 22ND

"Nice," I said, snapping a picture of it with my phone and posting it on Instagram. "Did you do this?" I asked. But I knew he had. It was a Pete thing to do.

Pete glanced down Main Street. "I hung them at the other shops and at the library, and the Senior Center too."

"Thank you. I say that a lot, don't I?" I blushed. "I mean, you're always doing such nice things and I . . ."

"You're welcome, Sasha." Then Pete smiled and despite it being twenty degrees outside, I felt as warm as if it were a summer day.

Once I reached the Hall's house, I stopped halfway up the path to their front door and turned into the yard. The snow was deep—I sunk in up to my knees.

I put down my bag and gathered up snow, packing it into a ball. Then I rolled it, and it grew larger and larger until it was the perfect size for the base. Then I started on the middle snowball, heaving that on top of the base when it was done. After I made the head and positioned it on top, I pulled out the supplies I'd brought from home. There were buttons for the eyes and an upside-down candy cane for the nose. It looked good. Two candy canes on their sides with the hooks outward and facing up formed the smile. That was a little more awkward looking, but it was the best I could do. And I made a scarf with a piece of tulle left over from our tutus.

Then I pulled out Kevin's top hat and perched it on top of the snowman.

"Finally!" Kevin stood on the top step outside the front door. "My hat!" Then he jumped off the stoop into the yard deep with snow. "YES!"

I laughed.

"Sasha!" He brushed off his snow pants.

"I'm sorry," I said when he reached me.

"You're sorry you stole my hat?"

"No." I hit his puffy coat. "I'm sorry I made things weird between us."

"I'm sorry I didn't tell you sooner."

"Yeah. It might've spared me some major public humiliation, but that's okay." I smiled.

"We're okay, right?" He picked the hat off the snowman and stuck it on his head. "Best friends?"

"Best friends." I reached down and threw a handful of snow at him.

It exploded on Kevin's coat. "Nice shot!" He tilted his head from side to side and tapped the top of the hat. "I don't know, I'm thinking I might not wear it. I'm thinking . . ." He lifted it off his head and put it on mine. "You should."

"No. No way!"

Karly appeared on the front steps, and I threw the hat to her. "Bury it!" I yelled, but she didn't bury it. She put it on *her* head.

"I'll wear it!"

We chased each other through the front yard, stealing the hat, until all three of us flopped down in the snow, smiling wide and breathing hard.

Later in the Hall's kitchen, we ate popcorn, laughing and trying to toss pieces into each other's mouths.

"I'm trying to figure out if Ryan likes me," Kevin said.

"He likes you." Karly picked a kernel off the floor.

"But how do you know if someone likes you?" he asked.

I dropped my head down onto the counter. I was pretty sure I had nothing helpful to say.

"There are usually clues," Karly said.

"Clues?" I looked up at her. "Did you Google that?"

"Yeah, that's how I figured out Ahmed liked me."

"Well, what are they?" Kevin asked. "Tell me."

"Does he call you?" I said. "Or stare at you?"

"Or try to impress you?" Karly said. "Or tease you?"

"Or compliment you?"

"Or try to make you laugh?"

"I don't know," Kevin said.

"Basically, it's everything a best friend does," I said.

"But it feels different," Karly said. "Like your stomach gets funny, or you—"

"Get a warm feeling," I said, suddenly thinking about Pete.

"Yeah, like sometimes I'll be talking to Ahmed, and I'll just start blushing."

I put my hand on my cheek. I was surprised, because I knew exactly what Karly meant.

Later, right before I went home, Kevin handed me the top hat. "Don't forget this. If you don't take it, who knows—I may end up wearing it!"

"Wear it." I waved it away. "I was giving it back to you so you would wear it. I want you to."

"Are you sure?"

"I'm sure. Ryan was right. It's perfect."

"Sash-aaaa," Kevin and Karly sang my name as I headed out the door. I was pretty sure it was my favorite sound in the world.

Chapter Twenty-Three
SHOWTIME!

On the morning of the Holidaze Spectacular, I was surprisingly relaxed. Maybe it was because Claire was home. Maybe it was because I slept late. Maybe it was because Mom made French toast and the three of us sat around talking and laughing, wearing our pajamas and fuzzy socks until eleven thirty. Maybe it was because I had my best friends back.

That afternoon, Claire drove me to pick up the cookies from Sugarman's. Pete helped us load everything up and wished me good luck.

When we were back in the car, Claire turned to me and said, "What about him?"

"What?" I said, blushing. I knew exactly what she was talking about.

"He's adorable!" Claire nodded toward the market.

"He is, isn't he?" My words surprised me, not because I thought them but because I'd said them out loud. "But we're just friends."

Claire arched her eyebrows. "You sure about that?"

Standing backstage, I heard the auditorium filling up—there was talk and laughter and coughs and a crying baby. And somewhere, I knew the director of the Summer Academy was sitting in the auditorium, waiting for the show to begin, ready to judge us.

Stretching, I lifted my hands over my head, clasped my fingers together, and arched my back, leaning farther. But as I stretched, the candy cane appliqué that we'd glued onto the leotard popped right off and fell to the floor.

I looked down at my leotard, and an orange pumpkin stared back at me.

"Oh no!"

"Shizzles," Karly said.

Pete picked up the candy cane. "It's okay," he said. "We can fix this."

"But . . ." The show was going to start any minute. "How? I don't have any glue. And we don't—"

"I'll sew it."

"Sew it?" Kevin said. "Seriously?"

"There are supplies in the costume room. Come on." Pete handed Kevin and Karly the box of props he was managing.

"Careful, try not to move," he said, pulling the fabric away from my skin, a threaded needle in his other hand. I smelled peppermint on his fingers. My stomach fluttered. He was so close.

I tried to stay still—the last thing I needed was to be stabbed by a sewing needle. But it was hard—Pete made me jittery.

"Is there a reason you have an orange pumpkin on your leotard?"

"It was cheaper than a plain one."

"Good reason."

Within two minutes, the candy cane was reattached and we were walking back to take our place next to Kevin and Karly in the wings.

"What's going on?" I whispered to Karly as I pointed to Ms. Kumar on stage.

"Special announcement."

Special Announcement? Exciting! She was probably going to introduce the judge and talk about the prize.

Ms. Kumar cleared her throat. I leaned forward. I didn't want to miss a word.

"As many of you know, this year the winners of the Holidaze Spectacular were to be awarded scholarships to the Summer Academy at the High School for Performing Arts."

Kevin nodded but Karly scrunched up her face as if to say, *huh?* There was something about Ms. Kumar's tone of voice that worried me. And there was her choice of the word—*were*. Uh, that was past tense.

"Unfortunately, due to the snowstorm and the rescheduled show, the director of the Summer Academy was unable to attend this performance. As she is not here to judge, there will be no official winners. I know this is a disappointment to our performers . . ."

What? No judge? No winner? It took a moment for Ms. Kumar's words to sink in.

"I'm sorry." Karly put her arm around me.

"Bummer," Kevin and Ryan said at the exact same time.

Shocked, I stared out at the stage.

"You okay?" Karly asked.

"Okay," I repeated. But I was crushed. There went my chance of ever stepping inside the High School for Performing Arts. Gone.

"Here." Pete handed me a bottle of water.

I took a drink. It helped, somehow.

"Can I have a sip?" Kevin reached for it.

"Sure." I handed it to him. Then I pushed aside my disappointment—the show was starting, and I still wanted to give my best performance.

We listened to each act backstage, hugging the performers after they finished. Before I knew it, it was Ryan's turn. From the wings, I watched as he wowed the audience with each trick. Then Kevin burst onto the stage and the two of them did a series of cool acro moves.

When his part was done, Kevin stood next to me as we watched Ryan's finale—he made Ms. Medley's cell phone disappear and then reappear under the seat of a random audience member.

"Listen to that," Kevin said, as the audience erupted in a round of applause for Ryan.

"They love him," I said, and I actually wasn't

jealous. Not one bit. "And they loved your acro moves too. I heard them going wild."

"Yep. I was pretty good." Kevin gave a thumbs-up.

Ryan bounded toward us, full of energy, and we all high-fived him.

"You ready?" I asked Kevin and Karly.

"I'm ready," Kevin said, putting the top hat on.

"You got this," Pete said to me as I followed Karly onto the stage.

You got this, I thought. You got this—the same words printed on the pencil my Secret Snowman gave me. I touched the candy cane appliqué, the one Pete had sewn on. You got this.

I was ready.

Karly sat down at the keyboard; Kevin and I took our positions; the lights shone down; and then . . .

Showtime!

As I moved through the opening sequence, I counted: one, two, three, four, five, six, seven, eight. By the second section, I wasn't counting. My heart and the soles of my feet knew exactly what to do. I felt the music, and it was mine. I sensed it from Kevin too. He owned it. This was where we belonged. This was how we belonged together—best friends dancing on a stage.

Breathing hard, we finished strong—both of us on our knees, our arms stretched back, our heads held high.

We'd done it. Given it our best.

Facing the audience, Kevin, Karly, and I held hands. My heart pounded as the applause rang in my ears. There were hoots and hollers and someone whistled. We raised our linked hands high. *This is winning*, I thought as we bent over to bow.

"You were amazing!" Claire called as she and Mom made their way through the crowd toward me.

After we hugged, Kevin and Karly came over with their parents for more hugs and more congratulations. Then we took a bunch of photos of the three of us—best friends.

"Sash-aaa!" Kevin and Karly sang in my ear and I cracked a smile.

After the Hall's headed toward the refreshment table, Claire handed me a bottle of water. "Sash," she said. "I'm sorry the director of the Summer Academy wasn't here to see you."

I took a sip.

"You would've won," Mom said.

"Mom, you're just saying that because you're my mom. Everyone was great and Ryan was—"

"True, but you, Sash. You were special." She paused. "I've been thinking . . . you should apply for the Summer Academy."

"What?" Water sprayed out of my mouth. "Seriously?" I wiped my lips. "But it's not STEM. It won't help me get into Tech Magnet. Plus, it's too expensive."

"They give financial aid," Mom said. "I read that over sixty percent of the students receive some assistance."

"Really?" I wasn't sure what surprised me more: the possibility of financial aid or the fact Mom had been on the Summer Academy website.

Claire put her arm around Mom. "Sounds like you've done your research."

"Plus, they have an outstanding high school program."

"Mom, I know."

"I think you should apply next year."

"You'd be okay with me not going to Tech Magnet?"

"You know, that was the right place for Claire," Mom said, tilting her head toward Claire. "But seeing you up there on the stage tonight made me realize it might not be the right choice for you, Sash."

"Definitely," Claire said. "Your place is on the stage."

"You should be proud of your daughter," Ms. Medley said as she passed by.

"I am." Mom tugged my ponytail. "Very."

I hugged Mom, feeling like I was about to burst with happiness.

"Congratulations!" Miss Melinda said as she and Big T approached me.

"Could you teach me how to do a stag leap?" Big T nudged my arm.

"Sure." I smiled. "Saturday."

"I've been practicing my shimmy. See." Big T tilted his shoulders forward and gave a shake.

Miss Melinda patted his back. "And it still needs work." We all laughed. "Sasha," she said, "you should try the refreshments. They're delicious, especially the cookies." She nodded toward the table where Pete Sugarman stood. "He told me the two of you made them. Together." She winked.

"Thanks for helping me before the show with my wardrobe malfunction," I said to Pete as I held a cup of cocoa.

Pete started to drop his head, but then he stopped

and looked right at me. "You were awesome." His voice was quiet. "I mean, *awesome*."

"Thanks." I glanced at his sneakers. They were clean today—no confectionery sugar or flour.

"I'm sorry you didn't win. If the judge had been here, you would've won. I knew you could do it."

"Thanks. But it's okay." And it was. Then I thought about his words: *I knew you could do it*. That reminded me of the pencils my Secret Snowman gave me, with the inspirational messages. And I thought about what Pete had said to me when I went on the stage—*You Got This*.

"Are you . . . my Secret Snowman?" I asked.

"Yeah." He smiled. It was such a nice smile—kind of shy, but one hundred percent sincere.

"Really?" Wow. Sometimes I was pretty clueless. "Thanks for everything." I blushed as I remembered each gift. "You made it really special."

"How is it?" he pointed to the cup of cocoa in my hand.

I took another sip. "Mmm, it's pretty good. You try." I handed it to him, and our fingers touched. A tingle ran through me, all the way to my knees. My knees! So *this* was what a crush felt like.

He tasted it.

"What do you think?"

"Could be better." He grabbed a candy cane from the bowl on the refreshment table and unwrapped it. "Here." He lowered it into the cup.

I swirled the candy cane around. The scent of peppermint made me smile. No—it wasn't the peppermint that made me smile. It was Pete.

"Now try it." He looked up at me; his eyes sparkled.

My stomach swirled, and I knew even before I took a sip that it was perfect.

Don't miss any Swirl novels! Read on for a sneak peek at *Cinnamon Bun Besties*

"I'll do it, Mrs. Choi." I raised my hand and to make certain that my teacher saw me, I waved. My heavy bracelet jingled like tiny bells as the charms smacked against each other. I loved that sound. It energized me to shake my hand a little stronger. "I want to be in charge of this year's Cupid Candy Cards."

I knew the job was already mine, but Mrs. Choi took her time looking around at the other students on the Fort Lupton Middle School student council. We were a small group of representatives from the sixth, seventh and eighth grades. Last year, when I worked on the committee for the Valentine's Day Cupid Candy Card fundraiser, we made the most money for the school in the history of the project. No joke. That part was awesome.

And so was the middle school Spring Dance. We used the money we earned for an amazing DJ! She played the best music, threw out lighted necklaces, and gave everyone these funny socks to slip around in.

No one said it out loud, but every representative I'd talked to agreed that because of all my hard work, I'd actually get to lead the Candy Cards this time around.

"Thanks for stepping up, Suki," Mrs. Choi told me when no one else volunteered to be the coordinator. She had a pencil tucked over her ear. Pushing back her short brown hair, she tugged it out and made a note on a pad of paper. "You can start by organizing—"

With a whoosh and a bang, the door to the classroom swung open. "Sorry, I'm late," Joshua Juaquin said as he hurried into the room and settled himself into an empty seat at the back. JJ was the male representative from my class who was also voted to the student council. "I was out on the soccer field with coach and didn't hear the bell," he explained, though we could all tell where he'd been by his soccer uniform.

He scooted around in the seat, tucking in his shirt, as if that made the uniform look a little nicer.

When I glanced over my shoulder at him, I could see JJ's cheeks were flushed pink and there were dots of sweat in his short brown hair. JJ caught me staring and winked. I rolled my eyes at him and quickly turned away.

"No problem. We were just getting started. Welcome, JJ." Even the teachers called him that. I think it took the pressure off everyone, since his mom was famous. If no one called him by his last name, it was as if they didn't have to treat him special.

"Now, where were we?" Mrs. Choi looked down at a piece of paper on her desk. "Oh, right, Suki Randolf will lead the Cupid Card Commit—"Our teacher hadn't even finished the sentence when JJ's hand shot up.

With a deep breath, I twirled a strand of my long black hair and closed my eyes. I knew exactly what was about to happen. This wasn't the first time that JJ had challenged me for something important. It was, in fact, the eighth time. Not that I'm keeping score, or anything petty like that.

"I'd like a chance to lead the Cupid Notes Committee," JJ proclaimed.

"It's 'Cupid Cards,'" I hissed under my breath. Then, louder I exclaimed, "Ouch," when I got kicked in the leg by Marley, my next-door neighbor and best friend.

"Shhh, Suki," she whispered to me.

"We all know why Suki wants the coordinator position," Mrs. Choi told JJ. "But, why do you want it, JJ?" She pinned him with her best serious teacher stare and said, "Convince me."

Instead of looking at our teacher, I swore I could feel beams from JJ's eyes staring at the back of my head. My skin prickled.

"Valentine's Day is my favorite holiday," JJ began.

I wanted to shoot up, out of my chair, and shout, "Liar!" But that wouldn't be cool. Besides, I didn't actually know what his favorite holiday was. I'd barely talked to him in the past three years.

I tapped my fingers on the desk in front of me while he went on.

"I've never lead a committee before, but I think I could do a good job. I have a few ideas on how to raise more money."

It worked like this: It cost students a dollar to send a heart shaped card and a lollipop to anyone at school. That was a Cupid Card. Buyers could send them to a friend, a crush, a teacher...anyone. Students on the committee got excused from classes so they could deliver them all day. The reality was the Cards, paper heart and attached candy, only cost 10 cents to make so we turned a 90 percent profit! Last year we raised over $300 to use for the school's spring dance. That was more than enough for the DJ.

"We can double our take," JJ said. "The dance this year will be epic! We will have a live band instead of a boring DJ, professional dancers to teach us moves, and get some awesome prizes for the best moves." He wiggled in his seat, slamming his head towards the desk, as if that was some kind of dancing.

"Wrong," I suddenly blurted out. I reined my tone in to a calm voice and told JJ, "You're dead wrong."

SW🥤RL

Swirl books are the perfect flavor: A sweet blend of friends, crushes, and fun. Curl up and take a sip!

Sky Pony Press
New York

About the Author

Laney Nielson is a former classroom teacher with a master's degree in education. She is a past recipient of the Cynthia Leitich Smith Mentorship and a member of the Society of Children's Book Writers and Illustrators. She lives in Plano, Texas, with her husband, two daughters, and a dog who thinks she's a cat.